In Search of the Perfect Ravioli

In Search of the Perfect Ravioli

A NOVEL BY
Paul Mantee

Available Press

BALLANTINE BOOKS ◆ NEW YORK

An Available Press Book
Published by Ballantine Books

Copyright © 1991 by Paul Mantee

All rights reserved under International and Pan-American Copyright Conventions. Published in the United States by Ballantine Books, a division of Random House, Inc., New York, and simultaneously in Canada by Random House of Canada Limited, Toronto.

Library of Congress Catalog Card Number: 91–91883

ISBN: 0–345–37261–1

Cover design by Donald R. Munson
Book design by Beth Tondreau Design

Manufactured in the United States of America
First Edition: November 1991
10 9 8 7 6 5 4

For George and Olive

And with appreciation for the following people who braced me during the process:

Sharon Daley, who nudged, cajoled, prodded, corrected, made me a Scotch, and nourished me from the beginning, and who taught me what an objective correlative is, but I forget.

L. Spencer Humphrey, who laughed and cried with me, whose knowledge and taste and gentle wisdom became a river of encouragement.

Maryanne Ziegler, the funniest woman alive, a muse for all seasons, who became the basis for a character in this book, and who'd better not sue me, and who will always owe me a lunch.

Ken Atchity of Atchity Edwards Entertainment International, without whose initial enthusiasm and guidance what follows would have become a letter to a friend.

Sasha Goodman, *the* literary agent, whip-smart and creative, to whom I owe the publication of this book. A planet, and although quite young and dashing, my mommy in a past life.

Joe Blades, executive editor, Ballantine Books. A special man, most generous of spirit, who eased me through an unfamiliar process with perception and enormous care.

Jonathan Mittleman, who read pages as I wrote them, and had the wisdom to tell me what I needed to hear.

The Felthams, Diane and Kerry, who computerized it all, and put up with my nonsense in the bargain, and the folks at Printing Square in Malibu, principally Ken, John, and Heather, whose work was cheery and flawless.

Anthony Costello, in memoriam, who said, "Write it."

Selma Lewis, Ph.D., who said, "Trust it."

Harlan Ellison, who said, "Don't let it bamboozle you; it's only a book."

And finally and fully, Susan Shaw, who shared the bamboozle, the hairy palms, the hugs and the fits into the wee hours, and who stood tall and quite beautiful in the face of my conceit, my doldrums, elations, and who has a hell of an eye for what plays and what doesn't.

In Search of the Perfect Ravioli

◆ ◆

I watched my grandmother make ravioli once, but I didn't pay much attention. I was eight. That Sunday I sat in her kitchen on a big brown wooden chair with a damp towel soaked in Epsom salts and hot water wrapped under my chin and tied at the top of my head.

Earlier, I'd been skulking around Beach Street on the lookout for bad guys, and I'd tripped on my chaps and hit the sidewalk. I probably would have ruined my Buck Jones cowboy hat if I hadn't broken my fall: my chin landed on my Gene Autry pistol, still drawn.

I'd stopped crying, and was studying the Phantom in the Sunday funnies, all but ignoring my grandmother, who smelled of fresh garlic and face powder as she created a masterpiece. Back then I took her culinary genius for granted. Mainly, I was wondering what the Phantom and his girlfriend, Diana, did at night after they finished *their* ravioli.

I spent the morning researching the availability of a ravioli attachment for the pasta machine I got for Christmas a couple of years ago, a contraption I've never used. I phoned four companies who don't stock the attachment, and a fifth who does, and they say it's no damn good.

I started thinking about my salad days. In the 1940s no one I knew who had a demitasse of Italian blood in them ever made fresh pasta anyway. They just walked down to Lucca's Delicatessen on Chestnut Street, where there were about twenty bins of the dried stuff, picked up a few pounds, walked home, washed their hands, and made spaghetti.

Today most people I know use a pasta machine about as often as they use the telephone.

I have this thing about the past.

I called my friend Maryanne.

"Guess what I'm doing this weekend."

"What are you doing this weekend, Peter, flying to St. Tropez?"

"I'm making ravioli. From scratch."

"God, I adore ravioli. With ricotta cheese."

"No."

"Whattya mean, no? Ravioli without ricotta—get serious! And speaking of serious, when are you going to get off your ass and write another screenplay, Petey? In your next life?"

"Ricotta doesn't belong in ravioli, and don't call me Petey," I said, ignoring the big question. "Besides, how the fuck would you know?"

"I'm a great cook."

"Tomato aspic."

"You are such an asshole. I want the recipe, Petey."

"I made my father a solemn promise."

I had, too. I swore I wouldn't share the recipe with anyone, unless I purposely left something out. He'd sent it to me ten years ago. Two single-spaced typewritten pages, as he remembered it from watching his mother create the original.

My grandmother had ravenous relatives all over northern California, not to mention five brothers and a sister who lived in the Bay area: Nard, Balto, Vic, Dino, Charley, and Clo. Some of them were stevedores, and all of them ate like it, especially Clo. I knew I was going to be stuck with enough ravioli filling to stuff a basketball, but I didn't care. The recipe was a goddamned heirloom.

I explained all this to Maryanne, but she didn't appreciate it.

"You have an uncle named *Nard*?"

"Had."

"Gimme a break," said Maryanne, cackling. "Nobody's name is Nard."

"You're not getting the recipe."

Maryanne is my so-called literary agent, and she thinks she knows everything. She's also the one who gave me the hotshot pasta machine, so that should tell you something.

Anyway, I was determined. My tennis had been rained out for the weekend and I was prepared to wash my hands and make ravioli. First, the shopping list. I looked at the recipe and checked the ingredients—one through twenty-two.

I decided to call my father in San Francisco. He's eighty-six and he lives out the Potrero. (Here in L.A. one lives *in* a district. In S.F. one lives *out the*.) He's also a little hard of hearing in his good ear.

"Dad, I've got a problem with the calf brains."

"Who's half-brained?"

"No, no, *calf brains*. Ingredient number eight."

"Oh, Christ, you'll have a helluva time finding those."

"Good," I said under my breath.

"Maybe at Petrini's up here. But only once in a while. I don't know where the hell you'd find 'em in Los Angeles."

"Are they an essential ingredient?"

"Christ, I haven't had good calf brains in twenty years."

"I'll bet. Are they essential in the ravioli?"

"*Over* twenty years. You know what they do with them

today, don't you? They put 'em in dog food, for chrissake. It's a crime. What did you ask me?"

"Are they essential?"

"Brains?"

"Yeah."

"Leave 'em out."

"Done."

"Nobody will know the difference," he added con-
spiratorially. "Speaking of half-brained, did you happen
to catch that horse's ass Reagan on television last
night?"

My father is very astute. I could hear him light a
Toscano cigar (it takes forever), and we launched into a
political discussion that lasted about twenty minutes before we hung up. I didn't have the heart to tell him my
taste buds had grown less sophisticated over the years.

My father took a long puff on his Toscano and blew
smoke over everybody's head. Then he reminded me
for about the hundredth time in my life that cowboys do
not wear their guns at the dinner table. My grandmother
smiled at both of us. It was okay with her either way.
Clo said, "Aw, the poor kid." And Nard rocked.

That's about all Nard did was rock—and yell like a
maniac when he talked, which wasn't very often. No
matter if he was mad or glad, he'd just rock. And yell
once in a while. Ever since he fell off his motorcycle,
Nard lived with us.

Harriet smiled, too, but a little too palsy-walsy to suit

me. The way some people do when they don't really
mean it, or they're talking to their dog.

My dad had invited Harriet for dinner the third Sunday in a row, which probably meant they were going to
get married and I'd have to move away from Nonna's
house and change schools. That made me sick to my
stomach. Just last week, Miss Wright, my third-grade
teacher gave me this hug that almost broke my ear off
when I told her about the divorce. It was during art,
and I was drawing a picture of my mother, who looks
like Irene Dunne. I don't know why I got so gabby with
Miss Wright all of a sudden. We'd lived at Nonna's
house for over two years and nobody else ever talked
about it.

"Listen to your father, Petey," Harriet said, smiling
like a stick. If she'd had an ounce of brains (sometimes
my dad starts sentences like that) or if anybody else had
bothered to notice, I was wearing my Phantom auto-
matic in my belt—not my Gene Autry revolver in the
sparkly holster. The Phantom is "The Ghost Who
Walks." *Not* a cowboy.

Nard yelled at the top of his lungs that it was the best
son-of-a-bitchin' ravioli he'd ever tasted, which made
me jump, and I lost a French bread crumb down the
bandage on my chin. I tried to get it out by shoving my
lower teeth up against the inside of my bottom lip and
grinding up, but the more I did it, the more the crumb
stood still.

"And stop making those faces, for chrissake," said my dad, who looks like Clark Gable. Nonna admitted that the ravioli came good, Nard rocked, and Clo said, "Aw, the poor kid" again. Harriet looked at me like she was smelling a piece of caca. If the Phantom hadn't put his gun on the floor, he'd have shot her.

My mother loved the Phantom.

Nowadays she'd meet me on the corner of Beach and Divisadero, as close to the house as she was allowed, and we'd go to the movies. Sometimes *two* double features. Afterward, during dinner, I'd read the funnies out loud to her and her friend, Leon. My mom liked the Phantom so much, she even asked questions.

My father liked him, too, when no one else was around. Like in the good old days when the two of us would go to Fisherman's Wharf and sit in the car, eating shrimp on a piece of newspaper. Or when he taught me how to light firecrackers on the Fourth of July. That was the year he almost blew his thumb off.

I knew they'd get married.

They were gone all day, and when they came home, Harriet was wearing an orchid—and my dad kept making toasts and mussing my hair. Then they disappeared. Two weeks later they came back from Mexico looking flushed. And we moved.

Dad assured me that the Sunset district wasn't that

far from Nonna's house out the Marina, but I knew that was a lot of crap (my dad says that). Fifteen minutes in the car is what he said, but I couldn't even hear the foghorns from my bed anymore. I'd rather live in the insane asylum. I was surprised I could still hear *Amos 'n Andy* on the radio.

Pretty soon my dad and Harriet got mad.

But first they got nervous.

My father started telling me over and over again that Harriet was my real mother, for chrissake. I don't know who he thought the person was who picked me up every Saturday where the N car stopped on Twenty-fifth and Judah. He kept insisting that the only thing *she* ever did was leave us. I considered that a lot of crap, too, and I think he could tell by the look on my face; before I knew it he was starting every sentence with *if you had an ounce of brains.*

Harriet got nervous about the way I washed my hands. My raggedy shirttail. That faraway look in my eyes. Stuff like that. The more nervous she got, the madder she got—and the more I knew who was who in the family, no matter what my father said.

That's when I developed the hearing problem.

Harriet would call me in from the street where I was playing, or even from the other room, and I just couldn't hear her anymore. I'd hear stuff in my head instead, like the distant drums of the friendly African natives welcoming the Ghost Who Walks back to his cave—

where he slept when he wasn't beating up crooks or saving Diana.

Dr. Gunn said my hearing was perfect. Probably even a little advanced for my age. My dad shook his head and Harriet got furious. She stayed that way for thirteen years, except when we had company.

I got mad, too, and developed a sullen expression.

Stoner Elementary was okay. School was school, as far as I was concerned, except for Benny Brock, who used to punch me. The best thing about Stoner was Heidi Rebholtz, who pulled her panties down for Frankie Dolan and me a couple of times behind the bushes. And Miss Lewis, my fourth-grade teacher.

Miss Lewis lived in the same direction from the school that I did, and one day we started walking home together. She wasn't as pretty as Heidi Rebholtz, but we used to talk our heads off anyway. She had brown hair and glasses, and she was my best pal for about two months. Until guess who found out. I think they called the school, because all of a sudden Miss Lewis started taking the long way home. She'd just wave quickly and keep going. Naturally, they made me promise never to walk home with her again. I think they thought Miss Lewis was showing me her panties or something. As usual, they had it bass-ackwards.

So. I developed a tic. Plus another disgusting habit.

Imagine the hand-washing problem, the shirttail aggravation, *plus* the faraway look and the sullen look.

And now on top of being pretend-deaf I was shaking imaginary hair out of my eyes and occasionally picking my nose and eating it. They went nuts. It was like living with two Nards.

Everything changed on December 7, 1941.

I'd been doing a lot of thinking about what Heidi Rebholtz had showed Frankie Dolan and me. Something was missing for sure. I don't know what I expected, but there wasn't really much to look at down there except skin. The only reason I was so anxious to go back into the bushes a second time was that she promised to let us touch it with a leaf. Also, I think I liked it that my boner was bigger than Frankie Dolan's.

Grown-up boys looked different. I knew that because I'd seen my dad take off his bathing suit. Grown-up girls who pulled down their panties looked different, too. I wasn't stupid. But how different?

I could just see myself asking my dad or Harriet. I'd have been locked up in reform school in about five minutes. So I went right to the Phantom and Diana.

Sometimes I drew stuff. I was very good at cowboy hats. Mouths were hard and so were eyes and so were hands. Forget feet. Anyway, I must've had about a hundred drawings of the Phantom in my top drawer, and several of his gun. I had Diana down pat. She had lipstick, long dark hair, and a neat nose.

The first and last time I ever drew Diana naked was that Sunday, December 7. I remember because it was the day the Japanese made their sneak attack on Pearl Harbor, and Harriet made one on me. Everybody was being more nervous than usual. I think my dad was mixing Manhattans in the living room. Harriet must have been mad as hell at the Japanese—because she acted like a chicken with her head cut off when she walked into my room and saw me crouched over half a dozen very nice sketches of Diana with no feet and hair between her legs.

You'd have thought I was the one who bombed Pearl Harbor the way she started swinging away, ripping up all my drawings. Then she did something that really scared me. She stood in front of me and started screaming, "Do you want to see what a real naked woman looks like? Do you want me to show you? Do you? Do you?"

Well, you can imagine.

I did and I didn't. Mostly I didn't, and I said so over and over again till I believed it. I was sure one of us was crazy.

My mom laughs louder than anybody else in the theatre. Usually the Fox or the Warfield on Market Street. Sometimes I get to take the N car downtown all by myself and I meet her in front of the Flood Building where Dr. Beltramo works. He's my dentist, and boy does he have hairy arms. Anyway, we yak through the whole double feature, cartoon, and *The March of Time*, which upsets a lot of people around us. Sometimes we go to the RKO

Golden Gate, where they have a movie and a stage show. We always time it so we see the movie in between and the stage show twice. A band, comedians, and Peggy O'Neal's Girls. Wow!

Then we walk down Market Street, still yakking, to Haas Coffee Shop and have lunch. She taught me how to go round and round on my plate so I wouldn't eat all my creamed chicken first and my vegetables last. She also showed me how to spit the raisins out of my rice pudding quietly and put them in my saucer.

My mom's friend Leon has a Southern accent, and he looks like Douglas Fairbanks, Jr. He likes me okay, but he has a picture of his own little boy on the coffee table in their living room, and it makes my stomach feel funny when I look at it. Leon should marry Harriet.

1. 1½ pounds boneless veal.
2. ¾ pound ground pork.
3. 1 pound hamburger or stewing beef.

It was still pouring. The last thing I wanted to do was market. Luckily, the Safeway on Sunset and Pacific Coast Highway is only ten minutes away, barring landslides.

I needed to check with my mother first. She's a wise shopper. Besides, lately I can't seem to phone one parent without phoning the other. Some nonsense about equal time. (I'm a little anal about a lot of things.)

My mother is eighty-five. She lives on the ultimate opposite end of San Francisco from my father—out the Marina—and makes the best beef stew on the planet.

"Rose," I shouted into the phone. Not because my mother is hard of hearing, but because if she shouts back in kind, I know she's feeling fine. If she responds like any other normal person in the world, I know she's depressed.

"Peter," Rose shouted back into the phone. And without a beat: "What's a nine letter word for *helicopter*?"

"Eggbeater."

"Eggbeater! Christ, I had *airplane*."

"Rose, airplane has only . . . eight letters."

"Honey, you know me. I'll make it fit. And how come you got so smart all of a sudden?"

"I did the same puzzle yesterday."

"No kidding."

"Ha-ha."

"In the *L.A. Times*? You know, honey, that's such a good paper. I can't even read the *Chronicle* anymore. It's all that crap about this one molesting that one. Enough already, like the little Jewish woman next door says. I mean we all know such garbage exists, so how about a little good news for a change? 'Course, you can't expect that with the Republicans in power. We need a war, honey. That's what we need to get this country back on its feet again. Lately, I just read the *Star*. And I have my soaps. Enough already."

Rose took a breath and I jumped in smartly. "Mom-I-want-to-buy-some-stewing-beef."

"Get good meat, honey. Stay away from Safeway. They buy crap. You want *choice*. Get the extra lean. The other is just crap, full of fat. People don't give a damn anymore. Your grandmother taught me how to buy meat. Nonna. Years ago. Look for the marble, honey. And if you wanted hamburger, he'd grind it in front of you. And if you picked out something that was second grade, he'd tell you. 'You don't want that piece of meat, Mrs. Russo. You want this piece.' It was ground steak. Look for the marble. People just don't give a damn anymore. What are you making?"

"Ravioli."

"No kidding. Your grandmother used to make ravioli."

"I know."

"Where did you find a recipe?"

"My father."

"Honey, he doesn't *know*. He never paid attention. You remember Mr. Gerrolomi, the butcher on Chestnut Street? You were too young. I used to take you in there when you were five, and Mr. Gerrolomi would give you a dill pickle, and you'd get it all over your sweater. Remember your little red and blue sweater that Marge Gavin gave you for Christmas? Marge *knit* that sweater. Great gal. Honey, go to Gelson's."

Or, I thought after hanging up, forget the ravioli al-

together, and march upstairs to the typewriter, and un-
block. Start a screenplay. Something. My mother never
had a blocked moment in her life. Why didn't I inherit
some of that? The only event that came close to blocking
Rose was the recent Asian invasion of San Francisco.
She took care of that in a Chinese minute by pushing
and shoving right back—and telling them to get the hell
back where they came from.

Rose vs. the Yellow Peril. An original screenplay by
Peter Russo.

Forget it. No conflict.

Or, I thought, I could take a nap.

No good. Too much conflict.

I'd been divorced from the lovely Jennifer—and brain
dead—for about six months. Dr. Toni Grant told me
over my car radio one afternoon that after divorce, figure a year of the willies for each ten years of marriage.

Subtract and divide and conquer.

By now I should be able to take a nap, Dr. Toni. Or
at least make it through the night without a three A.M.
Scotch and a long look at the hot pictures I took of
Jennifer in a Carmel Valley motel.

I'd married Jen for her legs and then tried to adjust
to her personality. My friend Maryanne calls me an asshole and tells me it's supposed to happen the other way
around. Maryanne also tells me Dr. Toni is usually full
of shit.

"Or," yelled my Olympia manual typewriter from upstairs, "how about writing a screenplay about a guy who enjoys a five-year marriage by screwing his way through an infinite number of terrific personalities, and still comes home horny."

Memories are made of this, not screenplays.

I told my typewriter to go fuck itself.

Just before I transferred to Catholic school, I stopped eating my snot and got ringworm instead. Several other changes were under way in San Francisco. First, my dad became an air-raid warden. Then my mom got a new friend named Bert, a motorcycle cop. Sort of like Pat O'Brien, but bigger shoulders.

Bert never went to the movies with us. He'd sort of roar into the garage on his motorcycle while I was being the Phantom and my mother was making dinner. They hugged quite a bit, and Bert called me *kid*. He even let me hold his gun once in a while. (At the dinner table!) He'd take all the bullets out and put them on a clean plate, then he'd let me hold the handle for a minute, as long as I didn't touch the trigger or point it at anybody. He was very strict about that. It was probably the heaviest gun in the world.

The neatest thing Bert ever did was drag me off one night—the night I happened to mention that Harriet had burned my stack of comic books because they were bad for me. He looked at my mom and his face got really red. He grabbed me by the hand and said, "C'mon kid." He practically threw me into the car, drove me to the drugstore, and told me to pick out as many comic books as I could carry. It must have cost him a fortune. Naturally, I kept them at their house. Eventually, my mom and Bert got married for a while.

Because I didn't want to get killed, I never talked about what a nice guy Bert was when I got home. Meantime, Dr. Gunn told Harriet that I got my ringworm from playing with the cat next door, and I got killed anyway. I never once put the cat on the back of my neck; but that's where I got infected.

Changing schools was Harriet's idea. Since somewhere way back the family was probably Catholic. Nonna said my grandfather was a Shriner, but I don't think they had any schools. Also, Harriet thought All Souls would be stricter than Stoner. All the sisters wore black. You could barely see them.

I'd pretty much decided on the spot never to draw another naked woman as long as I lived. And never to think about one, either, until I was very old.

Pretty soon I changed my mind.

My ringworm didn't hurt nearly as much as the medicine Dr. Gunn gave Harriet to cure it. And she had to apply it daily, too. Every morning before school, while she was still in her nubby blue bathrobe, we'd go into the bathroom. I'd bend down, and she'd put this ointment on a piece of cotton and rub it on the back of my neck. It stung ten times worse than iodine—she didn't even have to rub hard. I'd just bend my head lower and lower, and I'd try not to holler, which didn't work at all.

One day, while I was bent really low, trying to duck the pain, I turned my head and I saw up underneath Harriet's robe. Well, you can imagine. She had a lot of brown hair up there, and I looked at it every morning after that, until my ringworm was completely cured. I liked looking up her legs. It made my heart beat hard. I was just sorry it had to hurt so much. Harriet almost never got a kick out of anything, but she tried to make a game out of curing my ringworm. As far as she was concerned, we were having a picnic.

I never got ringworm again. I kept on playing with the cat, too, so Dr. Gunn was wrong.

Since I couldn't see Miss Lewis again anyway, changing schools didn't bother me too much. Except I think All Souls was built for kids who were problems to their parents. As punishment, the students were forced to be religious all the time. That didn't make my very happy.

I'd never met a religious person before, especially one who was in the fifth grade. That's why I kind of expected Catholic-school kids to look different. That wasn't true. Sure, they wore chains with medals around their necks and prayed till they were blue in the face with their eyes closed, but otherwise they looked just fine. Except Rita Repetto and Patsy Chumo, who had mustaches like my dad. I'm exaggerating a little.

Boy, did we pray a lot. Now I'm not exaggerating.

Every five minutes we'd stand up by our desks. We prayed for our moms and dads and aunts and uncles, and all the servicemen. We prayed for the pagan babies who were going to limbo because they didn't believe in Jesus, and for the conversion of all the communists to the Catholic Church. And sometimes, just as an apology because we'd offended God. We even prayed for Lucifer—that he'd change his mind and try to come back up to heaven. (He was about the same rank as Michael the Archangel when he was there, but he thought he knew it all, so that's why he went to hell.) We prayed for everybody, I guess, except Hitler and Hirohito. I used to draw them, though, during geography.

The longest prayer in school was the Angelus, which we repeated every day before lunch. We did some of it standing and some of it kneeling down. Sister would say, "The Angel of the Lord declared unto Mary." And we'd say, "And she was conceived by the Holy Ghost." And that was only the beginning. Up again, down again for about an hour. I didn't know what the heck we were talking about, so I just moved my lips and watched Nadine McNulty, who possessed the prettiest hair in the class—and sat next to me because she was tall. Her eyes were closed, though, so it was okay to stare.

At first I was scared stiff of every teacher in the school. No wonder. They all wore black hoods over their heads and robes that almost touched the floor, plus old-lady lace-up shoes. Not to mention big black beads that hung by their sides with Jesus Christ hooked on the end, nailed to his cross. Which really forces you to pay attention.

Also, sisters aren't allowed to smoke or drink Manhattans or wear lipstick or perfume either, so they all smell like cloth and have bad breath. With one exception.

Sister Mary Boniface, my fifth-grade teacher, had nice breath. She was also probably the prettiest sister in the whole Catholic religion. You could tell she liked the kids, too. She joked and laughed with the ones who weren't so shy. It made everybody smile and made it easier to learn fractions, which probably didn't even exist at Stoner. We even had homework.

One day Sister Mary Boniface read my composition to the whole class. It was about a car accident I saw on Scott Street just before my mom and dad got a divorce. I described how a lady ran out of one of the cars screaming. After her recitation, Sister came right up to me and handed my composition back with a big *A* on it. Then she looked me in the eye—hers were blue, by the way—and smiled and shook her finger at me like she was pretend scolding. "Keep writing, young man," she said. Sister did it in such a funny way, she almost made me cry. And in front of Nadine McNulty, of all people.

Anyway, that's when I started writing true-to-life stories. Harriet would have dropped dead if she knew I was having fun in school.

4. Eight or ten slices of Italian salami.
5. Four or five slices of prosciutto. By all means, imported.
6. Two Italian sausages, or calabrese (mild). Don't use the hot variety, for chrissake.

My father has lost no fire over the years. On the contrary, he's gained some. Sometimes I phone him just to hear him get incensed over insignificant matters. That's how he stays hot. He accepts his arthritis and his pacemaker (pacesetter, he calls it) as facts of life, but he goes bananas because Sugar Ray Leonard won't retire, for chrissake.

◆ ◆ ◆

My dad's name is Dominic. Like Dominic DiMaggio, only my dad doesn't play baseball. He plays handball and swims at the Y, and everybody has to keep quiet at the dinner table when he listens to the fights. Which is okay by me, because dinner is usually where we have our real fights when the radio isn't on. He doesn't hit me or anything. He just bangs his fist on the table.

Harriet growls during dinner.

For one thing, she hates the way I do my chores, especially how I clean the kitchen. And also the way I eat. She says I snort. But what she really hates is when I say I'm sorry. She always wails, "Don't you pacify *me.*"

She's not stupid. She knows I'm not too sure what I'm sorry about, even though I say it all the time, and that's what drives her even crazier. It's pretty confusing, so I usually say I'm sorry again and she goes bananas, and I start shaking my head all over the place. That's when my dad yells, "Jesus H. Christ" (I don't know what the *H* stands for) and bangs his fist on the table, and all the plates jump. It'd be pretty funny if you saw it in a movie.

I don't know whether my dad is mad at everybody or just me. Or just my mom for getting married. He never gets mad at Harriet when we're having dinner. When I'm supposed to be asleep, though, they yell at each other in their bedroom. I try to listen to see if they're getting a divorce. It kind of scares me and thrills me at the same time. Sometimes I rub myself against the sheets and finally go to sleep. My dad wakes me up in the morning when he goes to the bathroom: he always hits the water and farts like a buffalo.

Harriet really gets jumpy after my dad goes to work. That's when you can expect anything. She calls me Lunkhead, or Lunky for short. I don't even know what a lunkhead is, but I'm not stupid and I know it's not somebody you want hanging around all the time.

My dad works for the Bank of America. He's worked there for about a hundred years, but Italians have a hard time getting promoted. You can became a head bookkeeper easier if your name is Howard Hutchins—who plays poker with my dad—than if your name is Dominic Russo.

He finally decided to change jobs about the same time I started to become a moron.

It all happened because I have this best friend, Bobby Jamison, who I let be the Phantom sometimes. He gets to stay overnight with me when his parents go to a night-club or something. At least he used to. He lives across the street and goes to Stoner.

Lately I'd been doing a lot of daydreaming about dirty stuff. I thought about Nadine McNulty. Now and then in class I got to look up her dress a little when I'd drop my pencil, so naturally she was on my mind. I also thought about Harriet's thing—which I saw during my ringworm disease. Sometimes when I was in bed at night, I'd pretend that Harriet's thing was up Nadine McNulty's dress, if you can imagine that, and then I'd rub. I'd also think about Sister Mary Boniface and what her titties probably looked like, but I'm not exactly proud of it. It got so I was rubbing every night. I had kind of a one-track mind, I guess, but I lost my tic at about the same time, which was good.

Then everything got worse.

Bobby Jamison and I had this game we invented. We'd play it in bed when he stayed over and when everybody else was asleep. First, we'd whisper about stuff and pretty soon we'd get boners. Then we'd take turns being somebody like Nadine McNulty, or one of Peggy O'Neal's girls at the RKO Golden Gate, and the other guy who *wasn't* one of Peggy O'Neal's girls would do stuff to the other guy's boner.

Well, she caught us.

I don't even know why she came into my room in the first place. It was late, and we were being very quiet. But the minute she turned on the light she knew, even though our boners went down really fast. Probably because we were on top of the covers and had our pajamas off.

It was funny what happened next.

I don't mean funny like telling a joke. I mean funny like something you never expected to happen in your whole life. She was nice for a minute. Not nice exactly, but she didn't go insane like she did when she caught me drawing Diana. She got sort of understanding all of a sudden. I think she got that way because she wanted to show Bobby Jamison what a neat mom she was. She did that with a lot of people. All she said was, "We'll talk about it in the morning." I couldn't believe my ears in a way, but in another way I could, because I knew she was faking. She's a terrific faker.

Then, almost as an afterthought, she looked at me. "Come with me, Petey," she said, as if we had this big secret. It was more like I'd just tommy-gunned her mother to smithereens and she couldn't wait till morning to discuss it or I'd escape or some dumb thing, so off we went into the hall, and she grabbed me by the hair and dragged me into the bathroom. I hate when she calls me Petey.

Anyway, that's where she got really mean—in the bathroom. She called me a queer first of all, which was pretty embarrassing, especially because I was naked. Then she called me a *fucking* queer. That's when the roof fell in. She hit the goddamn ceiling because I made her say fuck, which I'd never even heard my dad say, and then she whacked the holy shit out of me. She was kind of whisper-yelling, wrathful, like the wrath of God, the way you do when you're mad but don't want to wake anybody up. "Did you hear what you made me say?" Like everything she ever did bad: *I* made her do it. I didn't cry very hard, though, because I didn't want to wake up my dad either.

When I got back to my room, Bobby Jamison was looking the other way and we just pretended to be asleep for the whole rest of the night. The next morning was Saturday and my dad was home all day, so you can imagine.

It was a quiet day, and I don't really remember most of it, except that it rained and my dad didn't bang his fist. He just wore this sad expression and asked me repeatedly if I wanted to grow up to be a moron who chases kids in the park. Naturally, I said no. (I wanted to be a newspaper reporter.) Harriet cried a little, of course, and they made me promise never to touch another kid as long as I lived, and to keep my hands off myself, too, if I had an ounce of brains. Otherwise, I might have to go to military school.

I think they phoned Bobby Jamison's parents and had a long discussion, but I'm not sure because I was in my room, writing "I promise never to touch another child" three hundred times. Guess whose idea that was. Anyway, it's not so bad if you write *I* three hundred times, then *promise* three hundred times, and so forth. It goes faster. Bobby Jamison and I never got to play with each other again, even on the street, so I guess the Russos did have a talk with the Jamisons.

About a week later my dad brought home this book about how children are born from a speck. He planned to have a father–son reading project. But he got bored pretty soon and we never finished it. He doesn't read a lot.

Every Sunday night we drive the Ford over Nineteenth Avenue, through Golden Gate Park, to my grandmother's house, and I eat too much.

We have to do three short rings on her doorbell to get in. She's funny about that. Everybody in the family was assigned a secret ring so she won't be bothered by strangers. (Except Mr. Spinelli, who delivers the cleaning on Thursdays; he comes up for a coffee.) Nonna gives me a hug, even though she's a little bit sweaty from cooking all the time and very self-conscious about it. She always smells like what we're having for dinner. She's also pretty fat, so she wears very loose housedresses. My dad kids her a lot and she punches him on the shoulder.

Nard always throws his arms up in the air the minute he sees me. "Jesus Christ Almighty," he yells. Then he asks me if I have horse manure in my shoes. (That means I'm growing fast.) I just laugh because he says it every Sunday and I don't know what to answer anymore. Then he yells, "Jesus Christ Almighty" again. And my dad makes Manhattans.

Sometimes other relatives come over. Except for my uncle Charley, who's the youngest and spoiled rotten. He lives at the Olympic Club, smokes a pipe, and has a lot of girlfriends. He also drives a Buick. And he reminds me of George Raft.

I like it best when my cousin Junior's there. He's older than me—and a really good baseball player. He could be in the major leagues. To show off his talent, he throws cups and saucers in the air and catches them behind his back. Sometimes he throws stuff to me from across the room, like a loaf of bread and I run for a touchdown, and we get hysterical. They never let us sit together.

You should see the table. We begin with prosciutto and salami and mortadella, which is like bologna, only about ten times better. Then we have bean soup or chicken soup or minestrone. Then we have spaghetti or ravioli, sometimes only a little. Then we have roast chicken or a rack of lamb or roast veal and fruit and cheese for dessert. (I forgot to mention salad, which is only natural because I can't stand tomatoes.) Nonna always says she's going to keep it simple this time, which is the biggest joke of the century.

The grown-ups usually laugh a lot. My dad tells the funniest stories of anybody. Or they talk about the war, and what President Roosevelt should be doing, and how come Charley got to be 4-F all of a sudden. Sometimes they yell almost as loud as Nard, but nobody gets mad. Just excited.

Harriet acts like she's Loretta Young or somebody. Petey this, Petey that, which means on the way home

I'm going to get several lectures about what a juvenile delinquent I was at the table. Sometimes Nonna gets this funny look on her face when Harriet talks to me. Like she's all tied up inside. If Clo's there, for sure she's going to say "Aw, the poor kid" about a hundred times, which drives Harriet fruit.

After dinner the grown-ups sit around the table forever and have coffee royals, which is coffee with whiskey in it and a lemon peel. That's when I go into the kitchen and find my dad's favorite blue ashtray—and he lets me hold the match while he lights his Toscano. Sometimes it takes two. Matches, I mean. The wooden ones. Anyway, I love it when the smoke goes up my nose. Then I sneak into my old bedroom and hear the foghorns. Sunday is my favorite night of the week.

One day my dad got fed up with being a banker, so he went into the restaurant business in San Mateo with his uncles Balto, Vic, and Dino, who got fed up with being stevedores. That was about the time I went into the sixth grade. My dad had to work late almost every night, which meant we didn't get to go to Nonna's as much, and I got to stay home at night with you know who, which was more fun than a barrel of monkeys.

The sixth grade is enough to make you puke.

I didn't get to sit next to Nadine McNulty anymore. She got moved next to Jimmy O'Brien, because he's taller than I am. He also happens to be the best football player in the whole school. He has wavy hair. (You'd think they were getting married or something.) Next to me was Victor Repetto, whose sister had this stupid mustache, of all people. Also we had to change teachers.

Naturally, we got Sister Mary Hitler.

IV

7. The skinless meat, white or dark or both, of half a three-
   pound fryer.
8. Two whole beef or calf brains. (Boil these in salted water
   for fifteen minutes.)
9. Any leftover meats from your Frigidaire, like some boiled
   beef, chicken, or maybe a piece of hamburger you didn't
   finish. (Fat chance.)

Anything that resembles a refrigerator is known in my
family as a Frigidaire. No matter which parent you talk
to. No matter what the official brand is. This is the one
my father and his uncle almost killed themselves hauling

upstairs into my grandmother's kitchen the day they said goodbye to the iceman almost fifty years ago. It's Dominic's hernia, Nard's water on the knee. It's Nonna's diary, the keeper of her most cherished secrets. Big, white, and cold is Frigidaire, and that's that.

Meanwhile, delete *two whole beef or calf brains*.

And good luck to me in my quest for half a three-pound fryer. Everything is 2.77, half of which is 1.39. Nothing comes out even. And better luck finding a piece of leftover boiled beef in my Frigidaire. Who eats boiled beef anymore?

Also, delete *piece of hamburger you didn't finish*. I'd rather put needles in my eyes than Jack in the Box in my grandmother's ravioli.

It was hailing in Malibu. Jesus. I couldn't believe my ears in a way, but in another way I could. It was so cold the night before that my potted bougainvillea, which had almost prematurely retired three hulks from Atlas Van and Storage, dropped dead. Appropriate. It was in my half of the divorce settlement. Jen got the VW Bug, the one she tried to hit me with a couple of years ago. It was on its last legs, too. All in all, I got the better deal.

I really have this obsession with the past.

The business about the car all started with the chocolate syrup that Jen spilled in the Frigidaire about three weeks earlier. I like things cleaned up right away. It's easy. Get a sponge, rinse it out, wipe it up, close the door, and bang, it's over. She knew this. That's why she left the brown glob on the second shelf till it looked like frozen shit. I could've wiped it up myself. The point is: *she* spilled it.

"Jen, you spilled the chocolate syrup all over the Frigidaire, honey."

"So what?"

"Aren't you going to clean it up, sweetheart?"

"In a minute."

Anyway, it was a miserable three weeks.

For one thing, I couldn't write my name, much less Act Three of *Cosmic Cuties in the Clink*. For another thing, I couldn't get it up. And the few times I did, it was sayonara in about three seconds. It's impossible to maintain an erection when there's chaos in the kitchen.

I could've killed her.

One day I couldn't take it anymore. I followed her out of the apartment on her way to Body Dynamics, calling her an unrelenting neurotic bitch. That's when she drove the Bug over a bed of succulents the landlord had cute names for, damn near taking my leg off in the maneuver. I jumped up and down all over Larrabee Street and updated the neighborhood on what a cunt she was. That just turned her on. She backed the car up so fast I thought she was coming back for another pass. No. She parked, swung those incredible legs out of the car, and whacked the holy shit out of me. A roundhouse right to the cheek. I dragged her into the house by the hair, took a left to the head, ripped her shorts from her body, and buried my face in her crotch for about twenty minutes—right there on the bathroom linoleum—till her arm hung limp over the tub, and she growled, "Fuck me, fuck me, Petey." Which I did. Later I had to borrow a goddamn chisel to clean up the chocolate syrup. I'll never find another woman like that as long as I live.

V ·

My dad is probably the slowest driver in the entire United States. Every summer we go over the Golden Gate Bridge to the Russian River, and the trip takes us two whole hours. Plus, we only have a Ford V8 coupe. (It's maroon.) So naturally, I have to sit next to my favorite person in the family all day long.

Most of the time I try to look out the window. The scenery is nice, and it's a terrific way to stay out of trouble. Unless my dad tells me not to be a marmeluke, which he does sometimes when I'm too quiet to suit him. I think it's an Italian word that means somebody who's afraid to speak up. So I start to speak up a little because who wants to be a marmeluke. And *that* always reminds Harriet of some crime I committed last week that drove her to distraction. Something that slipped her mind till this very minute. Then I *really* feel like a marmeluke, whatever it means. One time I just ate a whole bag of potato chips and got carsick.

You can tell when we're getting close to the Russian River. Everything gets green and brown outside and starts to smell like redwood trees, which are pretty extinct in San Francisco. Also, when we're almost there, my dad usually sings "Happy Days Are Here Again." (He's a very good singer.) And he starts to light a Toscano—till Harriet reminds him that we're in the car, as if he hadn't been aware of it for the last two hours.

We stay at a cabin in Monte Rio, which is probably the smallest town ever invented. It doesn't even have a movie. (You have to go to Guerneville.) As a trade-off, though, we have the best beach—probably in the whole river. Every day we go to Big Sandy, the largest recreational area for miles around. They have floats and a diving tower and a place that makes the biggest hamburgers and has Gene Krupa on the jukebox. Unfortunately, it burns your feet to get there because the sand is so hot, but who cares? At night they have a campfire with marshmallows and a talent show. Then you have to use a flashlight to get home. Monte Rio is very quiet at night, except for the crickets and the Pink Elephant, where kids aren't allowed.

Anyway, we get to stay for two weeks, and I just make it my beeswax to stay out of Harriet's way as much as possible and not to drive her to distraction, which almost never works.

I did two really stupid things. Really stupid.

First of all, there's this neat general store in the middle of town, where you can buy almost anything. And the owners are very friendly. We go in there a lot every year, and they always say I'm growing like a weed. It's called Torr's. Anyway, I stole some gum. Don't ask me why I did it. A pack of Doublemint, which was probably the absolute dumbest thing I ever did in my whole life up to then. Especially since I had about seventy-five cents in my pocket, which was Harriet's change from the beach towels I just bought. If I had an ounce of brains, I'd have asked her first, and she probably would have said sure. She wasn't some monster that deprived me of food or anything. Besides, it only costs a nickel. Don't ask me why I did it. I don't even know.

When it comes to counting change, Harriet's a whiz. I didn't even get a chance to chew the damn gum. The pack just fell out of my pocket while she was counting her money and giving me hell for bringing home the wrong towels. Bang, right on the kitchen floor. Well, you can imagine. She asked me about six million questions at the top of her lungs, then she called me a goddamn thief. Which I was, I guess, but I think gum is just a venial sin. I didn't exactly steal somebody's bike.

But still. Talk about embarrassing. My dad's part of my punishment was forcing me to take back the gum. He got this very serious look on his face and made me promise never to do it again. And I had to give it back to *Claire* of all people, the lady at the candy-and-chewing-gum counter who knew me since I was a baby practically. Lucky for me she was very understanding about it. I could hardly look at her the rest of the vacation. Talk about embarrassing.

Harriet's part of my punishment was something nobody ever heard of before. I couldn't believe my ears at first, it was so different. She told me to take off my trousers and kneel on this raw rice in the corner for half an hour. In the kitchen of all places, which is linoleum. (Practically everything is in Monte Rio.) She wasn't kidding either. She said it was a punishment her mom and dad brought back from the old country, believe it or not. Like some people bring back recipes or family photographs.

Fortunately, Harriet's recipe didn't demolish my knees—because when she left the kitchen I jiggled around so that part of me was on the linoleum instead of the rice. Then when that got boring, I shifted the other way. Sometimes you have to figure things out for yourself. Even so. It's a pretty fabulous view, too. To stick your nose in the corner of the kitchen till the timer goes off, which takes forever because you can't even see it unless you turn around, and naturally that's against the rules. What a lamebrain punishment. Try it with your pants down if you want to feel like the biggest marmeluke in the world. Harriet's parents were from Poland or someplace and they were both dead, which was okay by me.

Anyway, the other really stupid thing I did was worse. I actually did it again a couple of days later. The same exact thing, only Beechnut from O'Dell's, where we get our groceries. This time I kept it under some leaves in this big old redwood stump near our cabin where I used to get inside and play the Phantom when I was younger. And I only chewed it half a stick at a time (which isn't like me at all) when I was alone in the stump, after I shook the ants off. Don't ask me why.

Sometimes I think I save all my really stupid behavior for vacation.

For instance, I fell madly in love with this Jacqueline from Camp Imelda, which is a very strict camp for girls. They only get to come to Big Sandy for about two hours a day. She had fuzz on her arms and freckles on her legs. I could see her from my towel. I didn't even say hi, for God's sake, and I had two whole weeks to do it in. That's pretty stupid if you ask me.

The swimming race was no picnic, either.

My dad happens to be the best swimmer in Monte Rio. He takes his time and hardly splashes at all. Sometimes he swims all the way to Little Sandy and back, which is miles, and he never even breathes hard. He taught me, so I'm pretty conceited about my swimming. He's neat to watch, but I'm fast.

One Sunday the operators of Big Sandy organized this swimming competition for kids, and I entered. My dad gave me a long pep talk about relaxing and taking my time even though it was a race. And not getting out of breath, and that's what was important. When it comes to water, Harriet's a big chicken. She just shook her head up and down and said something brilliant like listen to your father. Anyway, I did—and guess who came in last. Guess who was looking at all these feet for the whole race. Guess who had this terrific slow and relaxed dumb stroke, and who could've beaten everybody if he wanted to. (Also, I have this really fancy racing dive, if you don't mind my saying so, and I actually had to slow down.) I didn't even understand it. It was almost like telling a lie. Worse, if you ask me, even though they treated me like a big hero for about a whole minute after I finally finished the race and got back to our towel and wanted to throw up. Talk about stupid. I'm boring myself.

Tootsie O'Meara looks exactly like Susan Hayward. No lie. Except I never saw Susan Hayward in a bathing suit.

I bet she could be in the movies if she wanted to. Toot-sie, I mean. Every guy on the beach is stuck on her. They're all over her like flies. She's a teenager. I stare at her all summer long every summer. I'm not exagger-ating. The reason I mention it is that she started me having a one-track mind again, but only because of the biggest coincidence of my entire life.

There are only about a hundred bathhouses at Big Sandy, which made it even more of a coincidence. (Bathhouses are little rooms all in a row and you get a key so you can change and keep your belongings there.)

I didn't even know it was her in the next cubicle till she yelled at somebody to be patient. She slammed the door, saying she'd be right out. That's when I saw the hole. You don't find a whole lot of holes in bathhouses, as a rule. It's very rare. Well, naturally, I stopped brushing the sand off my knees and got quiet as a mouse. And then I bent down and peeked. Who wouldn't? Boy, oh boy. What a coincidence. It could have been anybody but her. It could have been my dad, or Harriet, or even Mrs. Fitzsimmons, who was a sum-mer regular and had a lot of hair sticking out of her bathing suit. (Mrs. Fitzsimmons looked pretty much like Lou Costello, so it wouldn't have mattered to me as much.) But Tootsie O'Meara! Boy, what a coincidence. Come to think of it, she could also have turned her back and dried herself off the other way around so I could only see her behind, which would have been fine, too, but she didn't.

Tootsie O'Meara actually took her bathing suit off right in front of me, of all people.

I couldn't believe my eyes. And her thing was really close to the hole. I could almost breathe on it. (Victor Repetto calls it a twat, and he's had a lot of experience.) Anyway, Tootsie O'Meara probably had the prettiest one in the whole Russian River. I decided right then. It looked like this chunk of gold fur you could almost rub your cheek on. I don't mind telling you my body just about blew itself up when she started to dry between her legs. And she took her sweet time about it, which I was glad of, even though somebody was waiting impatiently for her outside. I admit, I touched my peter, too. (I know it's the same as my name, but I don't appreciate jokes about it.) Why not? Nobody was looking. I was having the best time and at the same time I was breathing so hard I was dying. Figure that one out. Also, I thought for sure she could hear me. Anyway, I'm surprised I didn't drop dead right there in the bathhouse. It would have been okay if I did, too, that's how hard I was concentrating. Except my dad finally yelled at me from outside and asked me if I was setting up camp. Luckily, he didn't know the half of it.

Well, you can imagine. By the time Tootsie O'Meara put her underwear on, I'd practically memorized what a twat was. And even though it made my nuts hurt every time I stared at her from then on, I was pretty much on the way to becoming a permanent moron for the rest of my life.

That fall I went into the seventh grade, and converted to Catholicism, which made life pretty confusing.

VI ◆◆◆◆◆◆◆◆◆◆◆◆◆◆◆◆◆

"Religion's a lot of bullshit," said Rose. I'd phoned her to get her opinion on Swiss chard, but I hadn't been able to slip the question in. She'd met a man the night before at Joe's, a restaurant and bar on Chestnut and Fillmore that's been around since 1936. My mother's hangout between four and nine P.M., since the Vietnamese bought Daddy Paul's across the street. She'd already mentioned to me that he was a retired army major, handsome guy, maybe sixty-five, and Italian—and that she let him know right away she'd rather buy her own drinks, thank you very much. Seems the major had made a tactical error during his maneuver, not difficult in a campaign with Rose. This old soldier stepped on a land mine in the first ten minutes and blew his ass right off the bar stool. "Bullshit, honey, that's the best I can say for religion."

"Listen, Mom, the reason I called . . ."

"Wait a minute, honey, I'm not finished yet. They give you all this crap about Confession. It's an excuse, honey, to do whatever the hell you want to do in this world, and not give it another thought. It offends me. Religion offends me. Men think they can do anything. Especially Italian men. And they all want to marry virgins! Get that one! I don't think they make that flavor anymore, do they? Then they go out on the street and grab whatever they want. Ignorance, honey, that's why I left Leon and Bert. Come home with lipstick on your collar just once, kid, and I'm out the door with the furniture. A lot of crap if you ask me."

"I'm sure there are some rational Catholics in the world, Mom," I said, trying to justify my own threadlike affiliation, which comes to my mind now and then during turbulence over Phoenix.

"Honey, tell me *who* is a rational Catholic. The Immaculate Conception, for instance. Figure that one out."

I decided against it.

I couldn't even figure out why I'd called. Rose didn't have a clue, either, so we decided on a continuance.

At least it wasn't hailing anymore. Just a fine steady drizzle. The kind that nourishes the gardens of southern

California and collapses the mountains on my street.
Where was I?

   10. Two large or three medium-sized dry onions.
No problem.
   11. Four large cloves of garlic.
Child's play.
   12. Several sprigs of fresh parsley.
Easy.
   13. Two stalks of celery, with tops.
A snap. But good luck finding the tops.
   14. One bunch of Swiss chard—stems and all—not the
       red chard. Must be green.

That was it.

Where the hell am I supposed to find Swiss chard,
stems and all, not the red, must be green, in Malibu?
In Malibu people eat nouvelle banana pasta with cream
sauce—all that new-wave crap.

I tried him.

"Dad, talk to me about Swiss chard."

"What's hard?"

"Swiss chard."

"Ohhhhh, a delicacy. Don't get me started."

"No, I want to get you started. Nobody eats it anymore. Boiled beef, either."

"Nonna's house. Every Tuesday night."

"I remember."

"November?"

"I remember."

"Jesus, so do I. Don't get me started. What the hell did you ask me?"

"Where can I find Swiss chard?"

"That's easy," he said with a tease in his voice. "I fixed some for dinner last night."

"Very funny, but I live down here on Mars, where people don't eat. They graze. Besides, I don't think I can find it within driving distance—and it's pouring outside."

"Just a little pat of butter. Pepper and salt."

"I thought maybe I could use spinach instead. In the ravioli."

"Or cold is nice, with a little wine vinegar. Better yet a lemon squeeze."

"Will you stop and talk to me *spinach*."

"You know, my hearing isn't quite as bad as you think it is. When are you comin' up?"

"Soon."

"Yeah, no, spinach is good." (When Dominic says *yeah, no* together in the same sentence, he means something in between.) "Not as good," he continued. "No substance. Spinach is like an unfaithful woman. It falls apart on you when you least expect it. *Capisce*?"

"Capito," I said, ignoring any one of a dozen possible inferences.

"Yeah, no, use spinach. About three packs of the frozen. Better than nothing."

"You can't find celery tops anymore either," I said.

"What kind?"

"Celery tops."

"Christ, you can't find those anymore either."

"I know."

"Christ, don't get me started."

One bunch Swiss chard, if available. If not, good old unreliable spinach.

VII ◆◆◆◆◆◆◆◆◆◆◆◆◆◆◆

Talk about carsick. When my mom and I go to Santa Cruz, we go on the Greyhound bus. I could puke just looking at a Greyhound bus. My mom too, probably. We only get to go for three days a year. It's some rule that my dad and Harriet made up so I don't get spoiled rotten. Santa Cruz is on the ocean, and you can freeze your nuts off, but mostly my mom and I talk ourselves to death.

She makes orange juice and scrambled eggs in the morning, and then we go to the beach. She'll say, "Look at that cute baby over there," and we'll talk about that. Then she'll say, "There's that nice boy you met yesterday," and we'll talk about that. Pretty soon she'll say, "What shall we have for lunch?" and we can rattle on for a pretty long time about that, too. We're probably the most talkative people I ever met.

We have dinner out every night and we gab endlessly about the other people in the restaurant or what movie we're going to see, and she usually says, "Don't talk with your mouth full, honey." After the movies we go to bed and have hot chocolate and take turns reading *Black Beauty* to each other.

My mom does this funny thing, since we don't have any privacy. She puts her nightgown on over her clothes and then she takes her clothes off underneath. She does it so fast I almost don't have time to be curious. Sometimes she says, "Pretty clever, huh?" Finally we shut up and fall asleep.

I started to go really insane about the same time I started to get really holy.

First of all, I already have this one-track mind about naked girls, even though I've never even seen a whole one. Like every day I look at Francine Dowling in the schoolyard because she jumps up and down a lot at recess and I get to see her legs. Especially when she plays jump rope. Volleyball is good, too. And I constantly look at ladies on the streetcar, and if they're pretty I take their clothes off, which is a game I invented to get a boner. I also go to the movies as much as I can.

Sometimes I look at the big posters outside the Irving Theatre, where I go on Saturdays by myself, and I try to look up the movie stars' dresses. I can't believe myself. Naturally, you don't get to see anything. It's just a stupid picture, but I keep thinking that maybe the person who draws the poster will make a mistake someday, and if I bend down low enough I can see everything. Like on Betty Grable, maybe, or even Shirley Temple. I admit, it's a pretty moronic habit.

Then I became a Catholic all of a sudden and got this other one-track mind. About Jesus. I think two one-track minds at the same time can make you pretty much of a mess.

For instance, you can imagine how holy you have to feel when you receive Holy Communion, which is a sacrament, by the way, and you have to be in the state of sanctifying grace.

The other sacraments are:

Baptism.
Penance.
Confirmation.
Holy Orders.
Matrimony.
Extreme Unction.

I had to learn all seven of them, and tons of other stuff, too, like the cathechism:

Who made me?
God made me.
Why did God make me?
To know Him, to love Him, and to serve Him in this
world, and be happy with Him in the next.

Which is only the first page, and it's not as easy as it sounds.

Anyway, Father Boyle used to come to All Souls once a week to help teach us. He told us about this guy in the Middle Ages who didn't believe that Holy Communion was the Body and Blood of Christ, so he snuck into the church one night and stabbed the host with a knife, and all this blood splattered all over everything, which taught him a lesson, and he got pretty darn holy after that. He even became a saint, I think. I don't blame him.

I don't even let the host touch my teeth. I just bow my head and close my eyes and let it stay there on the roof of my mouth, and try to make it last all the way through "Oh Lord, I Am Not Worthy." Then I go to bed at night and jack off. That sounds pretty insane to me.

Besides it's a mortal sin. And even though Christ already got nailed to the cross because he knew all along you were going to do it, you still don't get to go to purgatory for a while. You have to go to hell. *Straight to hell* if you die before you repent. Pope Pius XII is very strict about that. You can sort of tell by looking at his picture.

Some other mortal sins are:

> Missing Mass on Sunday.
> Eating meat on Friday.
> Murder.

Anyway, there's more, but the best way to get rid of a sin is to confess it to Father Boyle when he's God's representative in the confessional on Saturdays from two to four and seven to nine. He always forgives you, but you have to wait a week and hope you don't have a heart attack. Sister told us that if you lived on a desert island or something, or if you fell out of an airplane, you could get rid of a mortal sin by saying an act of contrition on the way down. (Sister says that actually happened.)

There are two kinds, though. Perfect and imperfect, and you have to say a perfect act of contrition or it doesn't count. You say the same words and all, but what makes it perfect is being sorry for your sins because you offended God. An imperfect one is being sorry because you're just afraid to go to hell, which I pretty much am. Anyway, the holier I get, the insaner I get.

Which reminds me that one night when they went out to the movies, I snuck into their room and tried on Harriet's panty girdle. I think that's a mortal sin, too.

◆ ◆ ◆

Naturally, it was Harriet's idea that I get baptized, which was a very nice ceremony, by the way. She thinks if I get holy enough, I might not have to be a convict when I grow up or become Benito Mussolini or somebody. Father Boyle poured the holy water, then we went to Nonna's for dinner, which was the best part. My dad made me about a half of a Manhattan, and I gulped it all in one gulp. Nard yelled "Jesus Christ Almighty" as loud as he could and everybody got a big kick out of it because it was my first taste of liquor and it really made my eyes water. Miss phony baloney told me to stop trying to be a goddamn big shot, but she waited till my grandmother was in the toilet.

Harriet's sort of a Protestant, I guess, but she never goes to church because she's too busy. She goes to about a thousand PTA meetings instead. No lie. If they gave a meeting at three o'clock in the morning, I bet Harriet would get all dressed up and put lipstick on and go. You'd think it was a dance or something. She even makes the cookies.

The nuns are always telling me how lucky I am to have such a wonderful woman taking care of me. Even some of the ones I don't know come up to me at recess and get this funny look in their eyes, like I was dropped on Harriet's doorstep and she was the Blessed Mother or somebody. By the time I started the eighth grade she was practically the boss of the whole All Souls PTA, which everybody thought was such a super-duper thing to be for a non-Catholic. You should have seen her on parents' night. Nice as pie. Talk about a big shot: she was head of the decorating committee. Harriet could probably become the first Protestant saint if she wanted to.

Meantime, if you want to get the crap beat out of you, just ask Saint Harriet to help you with your homework. Ha-ha. I'm exaggerating. A little bit, anyway. She likes to help, but only for about five minutes, then she gets jumpy if you don't understand right away. And if you still don't understand, she goes tutti-frutti, and you could get a whack on the noggin if you're not careful. I like to be in my room alone at night and daydream, but she's got eyes in back of her head.

My dad doesn't go to church either. Mainly because he's just too tired from the restaurant business.

He's lucky. He gets to stay out late and have a lot of laughs and a few drinks with his uncles after they close up. When I'm eighteen I'm supposed to be a busboy, but that's about fifty years from now, if I'm even alive. He's not so darn lucky on his days off, though. That's when he and Harriet fight—about how high to hang the mirror in the hall, for instance. They practically kill each other, and guess who always gives in. My dad's like me. It makes you sick. Anyway, the name of the restaurant is Villa Paisan.

I think having a few drinks would be fun if it didn't

taste so rotten. Everybody jokes around and they wear high heels and stuff. When nobody's home, I pretend. I go into the cupboard and get a Manhattan glass. It's got a stem, and I fill it with juice from the dill pickles in the other cupboard. It tastes almost as bad as a Manhattan. I double-dare you to gulp it. Then I get this piece of paper and roll it up like a cigarette and I play like I'm Humphrey Bogart being sophisticated. Pretty stupid. Especially because I'm supposed to be vacuuming the living room instead of flirting with Ingrid Bergman or Ida Lupino.

Sometimes I go into their room. A couple of times I even took some underwear back to my room and pretended I was rubbing up against Harriet and she liked it. Now that's really queer. She's sort of attractive, I guess, when she dresses up and takes her glasses off, but of all people. After I finish I feel like the biggest A-hole in the world. I wish my dad would just punch her in the face.

Being Catholic can be great, though, especially when I contemplate becoming a priest, which I do sometimes. They have a pretty neat life. They say Mass and hear confessions and get to play golf once a week.

The Church says you can live three kinds of ways:

1. A religious vocation, which really makes God happy.

2. Get married and have a lot of children, which makes Him happy, too. Or,

3. Live a life of blessed singleness, which is sort of like my uncle Charley who lives at the Olympic Club, and probably third best—but Charley has more fun than anybody. He has a new Buick these days.

I think it might be easier to get into heaven if you're a priest. It would be hard to do insane stuff all the time if you said Mass every morning, but I'm not sure. Priests have nice cars, too. Father Boyle has an almost new DeSoto.

I really do wish he'd punch her just once.

VIII

One night a few years ago Dominic heard the sound from his television set coming out of the risotto Milanese he had simmering in the oven. Doris Day. "It's Magic."

He also began having an almost nonstop open house for a crowd of strangers in his studio apartment.

Around three A.M. every morning they'd come in through the window of his second-story walk-up, perch on the stove or the Frigidaire, and visit. Nice people, too. Hell of a congenial group. They never said much, though, and only hung around till he turned on the light to take a leak. Then bingo. Out the closed window. The night Harriet joined them on the top leaf of the schefflera and gave him hell again for the mirror in the hall is the night I flew to San Francisco.

My father speaks English as if he teaches it. But he has a hard time these days—in fact he's downright grouchy—with any accent that isn't Italian. So when young Dr. Macadangdang bent over the gurney and welcomed the old man's good ear to Kysal Hospiter instead of Kaiser Hospital, Dominic assumed the world had the d.t.'s and he was fine, for chrissake.

Nevertheless.

The best convalescent home smells like equal parts Jergens Lotion and urine. Its chambers are overpopulated with slack jaws and eyes that focus on their own backside. Generally, it's a place where the dead continue.

Not so for Dominic Russo in 34B.

Oh sure, for the first month he was there he was doing play-by-play for the 49ers who kicked off in the hallway every morning. But by the second month he cut back to merely enjoying the game. By the third, he gave up hallway football altogether. The problem was they didn't know how to make a decent Manhattan at Hillhaven.

The camel's back broke the day he got two phone calls at the same time on adjacent pay phones in the corridor next to his room. One was from a doctor at Kysal who wanted to monitor the impulses on his "pacesetter" over the phone. Which he did. The other was from Angelo Pellegrini, who wanted the recipe for chicken and polenta over the phone. Which he got. In biblical detail. Simultaneously. Dominic even had the wit to leave something important out, a family trait. He was stark raving sane.

The family drinks.

Rose likes her Canadian Club and tall water, maximum two. Okay, three. And ever since the TV got fixed Dominic puts away a case of Classic Coke a week. I prefer a light Scotch after five. But on very rare occasions things go better with Percodan. It's as substantial as Swiss chard and harder to come by than calf brains.

I had to jump up and down and pout to get my dentist to prescribe it after he diagnosed my abscess last summer. He wanted to give me that codeine crap. Keep the pain and lose your lunch—that philosophy. He finally coughed up all of three pills. Anyway, I popped one and proceeded to get gabby and horny, thereby becoming the happiest person in the universe in about ten minutes. What abscess?

I keep the leftovers upstairs near my typewriter. Nice for a rainy day.

"I double-dare you to sit down and look me in the eye," whispered my Olympia manual as I reached around it into my desk drawer. She hates to be ignored.

"Not ready," I mumbled. "Get off my back."

"Chickenshit."

"Shut up. I'm going shopping."

15. A pinch of nutmeg.
16. Rosemary—mixed ITALIAN herbs—I feel rosemary should predominate.

Yeah, but how much?

17. A little oregano.

How little?

How little we know, ta-dum . . .

How much to discover . . .

Nobody sings it like Frank. In olden times Jennifer and I used to keep our grass in a little oregano jar. Smart. Who'd ever suspect, except every eight-year-old in Los Angeles? She was a lousy cook, Jen, but she knocked out a tuna casserole oregano one night that put me on the spice rack for the rest of the evening. The rest of my life. Forget it. Not good for me to think about it. What we did was get on the phones after dinner. Hers and mine. To each other. From different rooms. I'll never forget it. Forget it.

18. Grated parmesan cheese—four cups.
19. French bread—five slices.

Anyway, talk about total communication. Fuck the dishes, that's how free I felt. We became these very cool, very hot strangers. Whispers. Innuendos. Moans that were sagas. It seemed like hours. Had to be. Probably not. Then we had this brilliant idea at exactly the same moment. I mean exactly. I dragged my phone all the way out into the garden, which was pitch-black, probably murdered a thousand of what's-his-name's geraniums, the landlord, and I peeked through the blinds in the bedroom window while she was on the other end of the line doing this slow undress number. Not a strip. A slow undress, like she was on her way to bed after a hard day in the United States Senate.

20. Imported pignoli—six packets.
21. A dozen eggs—maybe more—depends on wetness of mixture.

Jesus. She really knew how to do it. Take off one thing. Get bored. Turn on the TV. Go for the blouse. Turn it off, browse *Vogue*, touch nipples. The works. And finally . . . *finally* lounge on the bed, cuddle the phone in total privacy, and make the most incredible magic . . . *you sigh, the song begins* . . . underneath those tiny panties with her body tilted toward the window and those legs all over the place. To this day . . .

22. Salt and pepper.

To this day I don't know how Jen got her panties down around her knees and her glasses off at the exact, *I mean the exact* moment of orgasm, and still managed to keep her heels on. I don't like to think about it. It's not good for me.

"Maryanne. What are you wearing?"

"What is this, an obscene phone call?"

"Ha-ha, just kidding. J.K. So what are you doing?"

"I'm sunbathing. Is this a survey, Peter? I'm doing what every normal person does on a rainy weekend. I'm reading the *New York Times Book Review*."

"Boring."

"What are *you* doing, still screwing up your grandmother's ravioli?"

"I'm screwing up my courage to go to Gelson's before the fucking landslide. Don't you think it's unnatural that we've never made love?"

"You and me? *Together?* You must be joking."

"No, seriously, after all those great lunches and insightful conversations?"

"My insight, Petey, is that you're a much better lunch than you are a fuck. Besides, hearing about what a dynamite number your ex is while I'm trying to locate your cock is not my idea of a hot time in the old town." She cackled. She always cackles. It's not very attractive.

"............................."

"Peter? Are you there?"

"Yeah, no, I was just trying to measure this phone cord."

"You're over the fucking moon. Now, shut up and listen to what I'm fixing for dinner tonight."

Pineapple pizza. That's what it was. That's what she spent the precious next fifteen minutes of my life describing. Pineapple fucking pizza.

"Pineapple and pizza? *Together?* You must be joking."

Sometimes I crack myself up.

Ever see a plain woman behind the wheel of a Mercedes? Or a pair of dull eyes rummage for a scarf at Saks?

Never.

Well, those are the people who shop at Gelson's. It's a quality market, gorgeous and expensive.

To make a long story short, I shaved, showered, shampooed, creme-rinsed, blow-dried, deodorized, moisturized, wedged my ass into my faintest pair of Levi's, threw on an outrageous sweater, leaned into a spritz of Giorgio, let a smile be my umbrella, and went grocery shopping.

IX

I made a novena to Our Lady of Perpetual Help that we wouldn't have to move, but we did anyway.

When I told Sister Mary Boniface, my old fifth-grade teacher, about it, she said that *no* was an answer to a prayer, too. So that sort of explained it, I guess. Well, not really. Anyway, we had to move to stupid San Mateo so my dad wouldn't have to commute all the time. Sister gave me two holy cards when I graduated from All Souls and told me that I'd always be in her prayers. Then she actually hugged me right there in the school yard, which is a pretty abnormal thing for a sister to do. All her black veils got in my face for a minute.

One thing I hate besides moving is that turmoil that happens in your stomach when somebody hurts your feelings or says something nice to you. You feel like a big baby. Anyway, I'll probably never see Sister Mary Boniface again unless I go to heaven. San Francisco is forty-five minutes away from San Mateo on the Greyhound bus. Blaaaahhhhhh.

So: I now attend Bonaventure High School.

First of all, it's all boys. Second of all, I don't know anybody. And third, you have to wear a necktie. And priests teach us. They're all Irish and pretty young, and smoke about three packs of Luckies a day. Most of them anyway. And they're hotshot athletes. Not every single one, but enough to have a faculty baseball team, which is an accomplishment. They beat the varsity all the time, too.

Father Lefty Cavanaugh pitches and teaches religion. I get to have Father Donovan for algebra, and he has almost a .750 batting average. My least favorite is Father Houlihan, economics and study hall. He's shell-shocked from the war and has nicotine stains on his fingers. He's jumpier than hell, too. Another Harriet, if you can believe that. Except he's fat and giggles a lot, but the minute he stops, watch your step. They let him play right field. (He's a joke at the plate.) I guess my favorite, if I even have one, is Father Wycoff, who teaches English and takes care of the library. I don't think he's Irish. At least he doesn't act like it—he doesn't have an athletic bone in his body. Baseball's such a neat game.

I don't know why I'm putting on this big act. Personally, I can't stand baseball and all the teachers scare the crap out of me, if you want to know the truth. Especially our principal, Father Greene. He's a prick and plays shortstop.

Things at home are a real bowl of cherries.

I'm getting hair on my legs like a chimpanzee—and under my arms, too, which is pretty embarrassing. And also you know where. Also, stuff is starting to come out of me when I you-know-what. The first time it happened I thought I was practically dying. But I can't stop and I didn't die, so I guess it's okay. I even like to watch it shoot now and then. That's about the only fun I have. I probably should have my own Kleenex factory. I'm getting pimples, too, and if I don't start shaving pretty soon, I'm going to have to comb my face.

I really shot up last summer, and I'm about six feet tall now and the skinniest person I know. I trip on just about everything, and my lips are too big, and I'm getting one long eyebrow instead of two like I used to have. I look like a monster. Dad says if my feet get any bigger, I'll have to have my socks tailor-made. Ha-ha.

And Harriet says I spend entirely too much time in front of the mirror, which is another big joke. I can't help it if my pompadour won't stay. Our house is nice, though, and the war is finally over, and my dad's business has doubled. Meantime, I can't even catch a baseball and I'll probably commit suicide before I'm a sophomore.

So I sent for the Charles Atlas course with my new best friend, Doc, whose real name is Dick, but they call him Doc because he's the smartest kid in the class and he's got a big butt and he's always dropping his books and losing his glasses.

Anyway, Atlas is this guy on the back of magazines who started out in life like Doc, so he developed the Charles Atlas course and got these fantastic muscles in under ninety days. Then he beat the shit out of two guys who tried to steal his girl on the beach. I'm not sure, though, because it also said, FREE OFFER. Turns out the only free thing we got was this pamphlet telling us to send in forty dollars. Also, Harriet found it on my desk. You can imagine. It took her about two hours to tell me how queer Charles Atlas was and to forbid me to even think about his course. I thought about it till I was blue in the face, but who's got forty dollars?

Then Charles Atlas did this weird thing. About a month later he sent another pamphlet to Doc. (I'm so glad he doesn't have my address.) Enclosed was a letter saying he knew how tough things were, and if we acted now, we could have the whole course for $28.95. Doc's so smart. He said let's see what Mr. Atlas does next month. To make a long story short, we got it for five bucks. Two-fifty each.

I did the exercises in my room after everybody was asleep. I didn't miss one night either. I hardly noticed any difference in ninety days, except my veins got bigger. But Harriet did. Wouldn't you know it. Old eagle eye. One day when I had my shirt off, she poked her nose into my room and jabbed me and said, "What the hell is this?"—as if she'd never seen a human chest before. God, she has terrible breath in the morning. Anyway, I lied to her, as usual, and gave her my patented innocent expression. Then I doubled my exercise program.

She's always poking her nose into my room. That's how she found all the Kleenex. I hide it, too, in the bottom of the wastebasket. But old eagle eye collects it like a hobby or something. She actually kept a perfect record on me for two weeks. Talk about wanting to drop dead. I'm sure she filled a shopping bag the day she drove to San Francisco and gave my whole jerk-off history to that A-hole, Dr. Gunn.

I said a rosary that she wouldn't tell my dad on his day off, but forget it.

I'll never forget it. He didn't even bang his fist—and we were having dinner, too. He just looked kind of tired and nodded his head and pushed his plate away while she raved on about how Dr. Gunn said I was *manhandling* myself. Sounded like I was punching myself on the jaw every night instead of the other stuff. And that what I really needed was for my dad to take me out in the woodshed—that's how excited she got; we don't even have one—and give me a good beating. Leave it to me to get that funny feeling in my stomach again. The one I hate. I just looked at my lamb chops for a minute and tried to concentrate on something else, but I started to cry anyway. Shit. I hate to cry. I'm almost six feet tall. Anyway, my dad stood up and took his belt off and marched me into my room and closed the door. Then he told me to holler like hell while he beat the crap out of the bed. What a couple of marmelukes we are.

X •••••••••••••••••••••

"**W**hat is a marmeluke exactly?"

"A what?"

"A marmeluke. *Are you wearing your hearing aid?*"

"That fuckin' thing!"

"What's the matter with it?"

"Huh?"

"*Your hearing aid.*"

"Oh, Christ, don't get me started. First of all, there's not a goddamn thing wrong with my hearing. For example. When I watch an old movie on television, I can hear every fuckin' word they say. Fredric March, Spencer Tracy . . ."

"Clark Gable?"

"Oho, unbeatable. The point is I can hear them clear as a bell *without* my fuckin' hearing aid. It's these new assholes. They mumble, I swear to Christ. Then I start fuckin' with these batteries and all I can hear is my goddamn false teeth."

I started to chuckle.

"I swear to Christ. What the hell did you ask me?"

"Marmeluke."

"Marmeluke." Dominic collected his thoughts fastidiously. I heard him light a Toscano. "A marmeluke is a guy who's making an ass of himself and should know better. Somebody who appears to be not quite all there. Nixon is a marmeluke. Our current president is a prize one."

"Would you consider a guy who went shopping for ravioli and came home with two pound cakes, a dozen doughnuts, a raspberry swirl, three pints of ice cream . . ."

He started to chuckle.

". . . a turkey, two salamis, and a bottle of Scotch a marmeluke?"

"I'd consider him hungry. Or stoned."

"Right. And a twelve roll econo-pack of toilet paper on sale."

Dominic's laugh is a salvo, and it hasn't changed that much over the years. A little emphysema maybe. No. A considerable amount of emphysema definitely accounts for the cough that follows. But it's his fingers that have really let him down.

He laughed, he coughed, he cleared his throat. He cursed his goddamned arthritis, and while he rummaged his lap and eventually the carpet for his fuckin' cigar, I browsed.

Boil brains . . . skip . . . Sauté #1 through #9 in olive oil . . . When brown add #10 through #13 chopped . . . Add Swiss chard (#14) after washing and cutting into four-inch squares . . . Add #15 through #17 and salt and pepper (#22) . . . When chard has blended into mixture and softened, take whole mixture off fire, let cool, and pass through a fine . . .

"Meat grinder?" I asked.

"There's my fuckin' cigar!" he answered.

"Good. I found the Swiss chard, too, but who the hell's got a meat grinder these days?"

"I do. Direct from Nonna's kitchen. So when are you comin' up?"

It wasn't the batteries. It was the volume control. That intricate little dial that requires nimble fingers and blind surgical precision to adjust once it's in its victim's ear. The schefflera needed trimming. The strainer on the faucet in the kitchen needed a washout. I'm always amazed at how short my father has gotten over the years. So noticeable when I hug him.

"What amazes me," said Dominic, "is all that crap that collects in that goddamn faucet. That'll give you an idea what they're putting into our systems. Rocks, for chrissake. And they tell you to drink a lot of water."

"Right."

"Bullshit! I got 'em buffaloed. What's the primary ingredient in Coca-Cola?"

"Water?"

"Aha. That's all I drink. Coca-Cola. And I'm convinced it's a helluva lot better for you than that crap that comes out of the tap."

"This is the best stuffed zucchini I've ever tasted in my life," I said with my mouth full.

"Nonna's," Dominic said with his mouth full. "She gave me this goddamn recipe forty years ago and it never came right. Oh, it was good. But not as good as hers. So one day I had a few chicken livers in the Frigidaire and I put 'em in for the hell of it. And I'll be a son of a bitch if it wasn't perfect. I called her and I said, 'Ma, do you ever put chicken livers in your stuffed zucchini?' And she said, 'Yeah, if you happen to have 'em around.' "

"Yeah, but you do the same thing."

"You're goddamned right I do. And don't ever give that ravioli recipe to a soul. And if you do . . ."

"Leave something out."

"Goddamned right. So. What's goin' on, anyway?"

"Well, when I get home I'm going to sauté my ass off for about a week."

"No, I mean what's goin' on, marmeluke?"

"I don't know. Not much. Maybe you and I should write a cookbook."

"Don't laugh."

"And leave something out."

We laughed.

"So where you staying tonight?"

"Rose."

"Out the Marina."

"Yeah."

"Good. How's she doin'?"

"Okay. Good. She's doin' fine."

"Good. What time's your flight?"

"Noon."

"So you'll stay there."

"Yeah. We'll have breakfast."

Dominic reached for a Toscano. I brought his favorite blue ashtray to the table and lit his cigar. He blew smoke across. I couldn't wait for it to get up my nose.

"How does she look these days, your mother?"

"Like Irene Dunne."

"I'll be a son of a bitch," he said, and he mussed my hair.

"He's got wax in his ears, honey, that's all," said Rose. "Your father has very small openings. If he'd go to Kaiser and get 'em washed out every six months like a sensible person, he wouldn't have to bother with a hearing aid."

"Mmmm."

"And it's his own damn fault about his teeth. Nothing against your father, honey, but look at these. Not one cavity. If he'd go to the dentist twice a year . . ."

"Could you pass the salt, Mom?"

"Dr. Spencer told me . . . you remember Dr. Spencer, I got a lovely Christmas card last year, his daughter, his *youngest*, mind you, is at Stanford, no less, prelaw, top of her class, quite a family . . . Dr. Spencer told me, 'Rose, I'm amazed at your mouth for a woman of eighty-five.' "

"Never mind, I'll get it."

"*Flossing*, honey, that's the answer, and brushing after each meal, and seeing Dr. Spencer twice a year, you don't have to be a genius to figure that one out. You're like me: I salt everything but my tapioca."

"I think I use too much."

"Salt? Honey, don't listen to all that crap they tell you today about salt."

"These are the best scrambled eggs I've ever tasted in my life."

"Nonna's."

After breakfast I changed the light bulb in the ceiling fixture in the living room while Rose convinced me that she doesn't know the meaning of the word *lonely*. She meets the nicest people on *Ryan's Hope*, for instance, and talks right back to them. What the hell! Why not? And three or four nights a week, Joe's down the street. That handsome guy she met at the bar? Forget him— she wouldn't have him on her Christmas tree. Exercise? She takes a walk on Chestnut every day. Yesterday she counted twenty-three Chinese or whatever the hell they were between Broderick and Divisadero. "Honey, I don't get lonely, I'm too active. Your father gets lonely."

By the time I got off the ladder, Rose had located several yellowed drawings of the Phantom, a couple of his gun, and a spatter painting I'd fashioned at camp one summer and all but forgotten.

As I stepped into my cab an hour later she opened her second-story window, threw me a kiss, and asked me if I remembered Santa Cruz and the fun we used to have.

Dominic and Rose haven't spoken a word to each other since the Allies invaded Normandy. Still, they manage to have a few things in common. The stuff of life.

When Dominic gets his laundry delivered every Tuesday, he can't wait to stack the fresh T-shirts directly underneath the clean ones already in the drawer. Shorts too, socks too. As soon as possible. This is the way it's done if you have an ounce of brains, so that everything will wear evenly, and nothing will be unhappy.

Rose's chest of drawers is a museum. Her panty girdles, top drawer left side, are a still life. Her hosiery, upper right, a monument to sculpture in an impossible medium. "Some people take care of their things, honey. Other people don't give a damn about anything."

Out the Potrero, Dominic's shoes stand at attention toward the Embarcadero. Left shoe on left side, right shoe on right side, heels touching. Space. Repeat.

Out the Marina, Rose's pumps brace rigid toward the yacht harbor, port on port, starboard on starboard. Both closets flank smartly to the right.

Dominic keeps a log of his bowel activity. Rose keeps one of everything she forgot to mention. The sight of the floppy end of the toilet paper gawking at him from underneath the roll instead of over the top drives him out of his fuckin' mind and makes her blood run cold. On the other hand, both feel pity for a twisted rubber band.

I don't have a prayer.

Am I supposed to be in repose, for chrissake, when I've got three pans on the fire, all different weights and shapes and sizes and colors, sautéing six pounds of assorted history, and the goddamn stove has small burners and big burners, and *nothing* is coming out even? Am I supposed to stay cool when I can't find my spices because Leticia who does the hundred in ten flat through this apartment once a week refuses to alphabetize like I've asked her again and again, and all she does is snarl? You could blindfold Dominic, for chrissake, Rose

too, and spin 'em on Fifth and Market, they'll slap oregano in your hand in scalpel-quick time. Now where the
hell did El Salvador's answer to Zola Budd hide my
goddamn potholders? Also airport security wouldn't let
me take my meat grinder on the plane. Bastards. I had
to stick it in belly baggage and risk having it wind up in
Bessarabia. All they saw was ten inches of cold steel
and a handle. Assholes. They barely knew what a ravioli
was. *Donde está my fuckin' potholders???!!!*

"Calm down," said a familiar voice from upstairs.
"Por favor."

"I'm not even cleaning up as I go along!"

"Shhhhhh."

"It's a family ritual," I whimpered.

"Just. Calm. Down."

"Yeah, but . . ."

"Relax. The way Dominic used to swim the Russian
River. One stroke at a time. No splash. Not too many
bubbles. Life is not a race. Ravioli is not a race. Take
a deep breath."

". . . . ."

"That's it. Another."

". . . . ."

"Good. Now listen up," said my know-it-all Olympia
manual. "San Francisco is a race. A race to once upon
a time. It makes you crazy."

Take the whole mixture off the fire—let it cool.

XI ◆◆◆◆◆◆◆◆◆◆◆◆◆◆◆◆◆

One thing I do know for sure is that I'm definitely not going to become a priest when I grow up. I made up my mind once and for all at Camp Marwedel, where I got sent for eight weeks so Harriet could get some peace and quiet. Camp was supposed to be a punishment for putting her on the verge of a nervous breakdown. Ha. It was only the most interesting summer vacation I ever had in my entire life. At first I hated the idea because I wouldn't be able to go up the river and stare at Tootsie O'Meara. And I'd probably have to meet about five hundred new kids I never saw before. And also I'd miss my dad. Boy, was I in for a surprise. I didn't miss anybody. I didn't even want to come home, period.

Camp Marwedel is all boys. Well, almost.

I was assigned to write this composition about it when I got back to school, but I had to leave the best material out. It stinks. Here it is anyway.

I spent my summer vacation at Camp Marwedel. It took a whole day to get there, and you can't even drive into the place. Once we got to Fort Bragg we had to take the Skunk the rest of the way, which is a little train that looks like an orange streetcar.

The Noyo Creek runs right through the camp, and Indians used to live there and fish for trout, which I did. They have a swimming hole, a craft shop, horse-back riding, and nature study, where I spatter-painted several leaves onto paper and gave them out to my family. And also a dining hall, where I helped out twice a week.

We had campfires every night with talent shows. One boy named Nicky Fasullo can sing as good as Bing Crosby any day of the week, and he's only twelve. He should go to Hollywood. Then we all sang taps, and went to sleep in open-air cabins. I never saw so many pretty stars in one place in my whole life.

A priest named Father Ryan came in on the Skunk every Sunday and said Mass in a little outdoor grotto. The altar and the pews were all made out of beautiful redwood. The Protestants had to go to the amphitheatre.

I spent a great deal of time at nature study.

Pretty shitty. Anyway, Father Wycoff gave me a *C*-plus on it because I forgot to describe the trees or to mention the locale—Mendocino County. Also it was too short. If it was any longer, I'd have gotten thrown out of school.

For instance, like why I spent all that time at nature study.

But even before that. Don't ask me why, but I went to the Protestant services one Sunday just for the heck of it, which would have thrilled Father Wycoff no end. They sang, "Onward Christian Soldiers" instead of "Long Live the Pope." It's a good song, too. I wish we had it.

Also, we had three Negro boys at camp: Eightball, Inkspot, and Sunshine. I can't imagine that Father would get a bang out of my sticking them in my composition, since we don't have any at Bonaventure High—or any other school I've ever been to, for that matter.

Sunshine is sixteen. His parents are very poor, so he has to work his way through camp by taking charge of the dining hall, where I help out sometimes. One day this neat thing happened when I asked Sunshine where the butter machine was—so I could make the little pats for lunchtime.

He stopped everything and looked at me real seriously—not stern or anything—and he said, "My name is David, David Snowden."

I smiled and said, "Okay, David, can you show me how to do the butter?"

Then he looked at me right in the eyes and smiled back. God. It could've been in the movies, it was so neat. Don't get me wrong. We're not queer or anything, but we got to be really good friends after that and went fishing a lot, when I wasn't pursuing nature, as he called it, but that's another story. Anyway, David taught me how to bone a trout and cook it over a little fire we built right there by the creek.

Eightball's name is Michael, and Inkspot's is James. The two Chinese cooks are Fred and George.

Okay, there was this girl.

Her real name is Ernestine, but everybody calls her Nature because that's the department she's head of. She's not some super debutante or anything, but she has a sexy figure and brown eyes and her ambition is to be Alexis Smith, except she has this chestnut hair, which she's thinking about bleaching. She'll be seventeen this coming October.

Her sister is Nurse Jane, a killer-diller. Laraine Day, I kid you not. Anyway, Nurse is in love with Moose, the lifeguard, and I think they do it just about every night of the week. That's how come Nature gets to sneak out of the cabin. She's twenty-one, Nurse is. Two girls and about a million guys. Hard to believe.

Anyway, I sort of fell in love with Nature. Reuben

Minchaca says it's puppy love because I'm only fifteen. He also told me Nature had a rep from last year and that he even made out with her once, but I don't care. All I know is I spent about three weeks learning how to spatter-paint a stupid leaf onto a piece of paper, and it was worth it.

What she did was sort of breathe on the back of your neck every time she showed you how to move the little brush against the screen. Naturally, I ruined about every leaf in camp, so one day Nature took me by the hand and put her tit against my arm and we did it together. Jesus H. Christ, I hate to swear, but I practically missed the whole leaf and got this fever all over. And she could tell, too. Pretty soon we weren't even spattering, we were just standing there breathing. I know she could tell, because she stuck around even after this little fairy ran up and tried to kiss her ass about some masterpiece he just painted. I almost tripped over the butterfly collection when she said let's take a walk after taps, but if you tell I'll kill you. Me of all people. Fat chance. I only told David Snowden. Well, I had to tell Reuben Minchaca, too, because he's eighteen and helped me shave.

I learned a lot from Nature, although I could probably be excommunicated for most of it.

It was nice for a while, our walks and our talks. She'd always bring a couple of movie magazines with her and first we'd lie down under a tree and look at them with flashlights. That's how she got the idea to teach me how to do a movie-star kiss, where you keep your lips open and wiggle your tongue. Talk about a new one on me. I didn't even mind the germs. She knew a lot about Hollywood. Her favorite was Errol Flynn. She was practically nuts about him. He's okay, I guess. I got a little sick of him after a while, but let's face it: I was the one who got to put my hand down Nature's brassiere and he didn't. She would've have let him, though, if he asked. I'm pretty sure.

You know what can really drive a person crazy? When somebody pulls a person's hand away and says we shouldn't be doing this when you're already doing it. I hate that. Except for the last night, which I don't want to get too personal about because it was pretty hot and pretty weird, too. She unbuttoned my pants is what she did—you could have knocked me over with a feather—and put her hand inside my shorts. I'm not exaggerating. And leave it to me, I forgot what pocket I put my stupid Kleenex in just in case. I said I was sorry, but that wasn't the worst of it. When she finally let me put my hand down her jeans—she did, I kid you not—I didn't even know what to do. Obviously, I'm no big Errol Flynn or anything because she had to hold my hand and move it around just like she did when she taught me to spatter-paint, until she finally got out of breath. The worst of it was I told her I love you while we were looking at the stars after, and all she said was that she had to go. Maybe she didn't hear me.

The next night she took a walk with Harry Barovsky, the big shot who takes care of the horses. That's what Reuben Minchaca said, anyway. He's no Errol Flynn either. Harry Barovsky, I mean. Take my word for it. I hope they're very happy.

The last night at Camp Marwedel we had this huge campfire, and Nicky Fasullo sang "I Had the Craziest Dream." It's his best song. It goes:

> *I had the craziest dream last night.*
> *Yes, I did.*

I know all the words by heart, but I don't want to go into it. Anyway, nobody sings it like Nicky.

I'll probably send Nature a birthday card on October 29th if I think of it. I kept her address. Don't ask me why.

XII ◆◆◆◆◆◆◆◆◆◆◆◆◆◆◆◆

I had the craziest dream last night. I dreamed my cock was in my pocket. Literally. I remember looking for it in its usual place—don't ask me why—and there was nothing there. Just a flat space. I don't know what possessed me to pat down the rest of my body—panic, I guess—but I groped everywhere. Knees, ankles, elbows. Zippo, *niente, adiós muchacho*. Finally, I recognized a familiar bulge in my right pants pocket. I reached in and there it was along with my car keys and some loose change. Thank God for small favors.

I woke up in a sweat about three A.M., went to the john, convinced myself I was all in one piece, swigged a can of apple juice, went back to bed, and fell right back into the same dream. I wish I could remember all of it. I should have written it down. I'm not suggesting there's a screenplay there, but I must be getting back on track because the first notion that occurred to me when the sun streamed through the blinds this morning was a how-to book. What do you do with a cock in a pocket? Interesting? Anyway, it was gorgeous outside after the rain.

Pass it through a fine meat grinder.

What the hell have I got here on the stove?

Veal, pork, salami, prosciutto, sausage, chicken, chard, celery, onions, parsley, garlic, rosemary, oregano, thyme, sage, marjoram, basil, nutmeg, salt and pepper—cold and sautéed. And I don't recognize any of it. Camouflage, that's what it looks like. Green-brown camouflage in 3-D, enough to disguise an Italian regiment, as if they needed disguising. And over here we have a meat grinder that appears to be a relic. I make it out to be a toy from the last days of Pompeii. It holds about half a cup of you name it at a time, and it has a cute handle that goes around and around and around. I'm looking at a meditation here. I'll be cranking away till Columbus Day, stuffing and grinding. I figure to be in a major-league trance by four, nirvana at eleven. No wonder my grandmother never said much. She spent half her life in an astral state and I'm exhausted from playing search and seizure all night and just not in a ravioli mood.

"Just a goddamned minute."

"Huh?"

"You want to douse that cigarette, put the coffee aside, and take a big whiff of that guck?"

"Are we doing deep breaths again?"

"Just do it."

". . . . ."

And time yanked me by the nostrils, did a bass-ackwards somersault, and before I could yell Jesus Christ Almighty at the top of my lungs the Phantom could almost hear the foghorns on Beach Street. I washed my hands (mindful of dreams), pressed a little bit of heaven into the grinder, and slowly began to stuff and crank and stuff and crank. The kitchen moved and Nonna said it came good.

XIII

Sometimes it's so neat to know about snooty stuff.

For instance, nobody in my whole family knows what beef Stroganoff is but me. I had it for dinner Friday night at the Cassidys' house in Hillsborough. Mansion is more like it. They're so rich it's hard to breathe at the dinner table.

I tried it on for size Sunday night at Nonna's. She'd never heard of Stroganoff before, but she was pretty sure it wasn't Italian. Nonna's trying to lose weight these days, and Dr. Herzog says it's about time, too. She's almost down to 190. Meantime, I'm almost up to 180 thanks to Charles Atlas. We plan a celebration dinner together at 185. Not Charles Atlas and I. *Nonna* and I, naturally. (Father Wycoff says my antecedents stink.) It's going to be hard for her, though, because the only time she doesn't talk about food is when her mouth is full. My whole family, for that matter.

So everybody sort of stopped chewing and got interested for a minute when I broached the subject of what I had for dinner Friday night. Clo looked at me across the table and said, "Aw, the poor kid," as if I'd been forced to eat creamed tuna or something. And Nard rocked his ass off and yelled, "Stroganoff, Jesus Christ Almighty!" Apparently he and Mr. Stroganoff were best pals from the old days. Nard's losing his marbles. He might have to go to the crazy house in Napa. My dad came closest. He'd heard of it, but he wasn't sure what it was. Harriet acted as if she practically invented it and excused herself from the table. My uncle Charley almost fell into his antipasto because beef Stroganoff reminded him of a joke he heard at the Olympic Club.

You know who was the only person at the table who knew what beef Stroganoff was besides me? Vivian. Charley's new girlfriend, Vivian Van Alden. She's a buyer at I. Magnin's. She knew exactly what it was. First she slapped Charley on the shoulder and told him to shut up, sweetheart, and then she said, "Delightful. Lean beef lightly sautéed. Onion, mushroom, the faintest touch of garlic, blended with broth, flour, and sour cream." She's so neat.

So I said, "Served over noodles."

Then she looked right at me like we were alone in a fancy nightclub or something and said, "Mmmm, was it divine, Peter? I'll bet it was."

I'd like to feel up Vivian Van Alden. I really would.

Feeling up is about all I'm interested in these days. I don't mean it's *all* I'm interested in. I think about football now and then, too, and I've decided that if I get less clumsy I should maybe go out for it when I'm a junior. I'd probably get killed, knowing me. I told my dad and Harriet that I was considering trying out for the team. Actually, I asked them if I could consider it and they said it was absolutely forbidden. Especially Harriet. I think I'm going to do it. I am. I just this minute decided.

I also think about, of all things, *Hamlet*. I can't even believe myself that I think about *Hamlet*. One reason is we're studying it. We already did *David Copperfield*, which I liked okay, but it didn't stick with me too much later. Doc said I reminded him of Steerforth, this guy in *David Copperfield*. It was kind of embarrassing because we were at the part of the book where Steerforth was this big hero, but he turned out to be a prize asshole at the end, so I don't know. Anyway, *Hamlet*'s a lot shorter.

I think about feeling up because I'm bewildered.

First of all, how does a guy stick his dick in a twat anyway? I don't think it could work. The hole is too little, that's why, and if it did work it would probably hurt like hell. I bent my boner a few times turning over in bed, and it didn't exactly feel terrific. Also, I'm positive that a baby can't come out of a twat. It's impossible. So they must do it another way. I'm just not sure how yet, that's all.

If I asked Father Wycoff, number one, he's not supposed to know that stuff and number two, I'd probably spend the next twenty years copying out the Latin index. God, I hate Latin. Cicero. Puke.

I can just see myself asking my dad and my favorite stepmother, "How come a baby comes out of a twat when I never saw a baby littler than a dick?" I'd be in Alcatraz in five minutes.

So maybe I could just feel up girls and ask them to rub me. That sounds jim-dandy to me, and certainly more fun than the way it's supposed to be. It's not exactly my life ambition to bend my boner all the time. And another thing, say it was big enough to stick a dick in, which it isn't, then it wouldn't be small enough to take a pee out of. It doesn't make sense and that's all there is to it.

The girl I'd like to feel up most is Yvonne Cassidy, but lots of luck. They call her Vonnie for short. She *really* looks like Alexis Smith and she's a little snooty, which is one of the reasons I'd like to feel her up, but I don't think she'd rub me even if I begged her to. She goes to Mercy High in Burlingame and she's the big reason I started playing tennis. I'd like to feel up Bobbie Flaherty, too. She's also very cute (Gloria DeHaven), and John Spellman who's the best fullback in the history of Bonaventure High said she's hot and loves to do it. But do what? See, that's what I don't even know and I'd like to find out for once in my life. I'll bet there are tons of hot girls at Mercy, except for a few like Mary Frances Dennehy. She goes with Doc and wants to be a nun. Poor Doc. Anyway, Vonnie Cassidy is the neatest, and I'm convinced it would be more fun to feel up a snooty girl than somebody who's already hot. But fat chance. Beggars can't be choosers.

How I met Vonnie was at a dance at Mercy that Bonaventure got invited to, but I only danced with her once because I started to sweat. I hate that. How I got to know her was hanging around Fitzgerald Field, which is this huge park on El Camino where everybody goes, and where I play handball with guys from the other side of the tracks. They're my private friends. Can't you just see me bringing Getulio Mendoza, for instance, home for lunch? Harriet would crap in her pants. He's from Guam. Anyway, one day Vonnie Cassidy walked by with Betty Feely, wearing shorts and swinging her tennis racquet, so we said hi and I quit my game.

Fate cries out, as Hamlet would say. Wheaties had

this one-time special offer where you could send in two box tops and get a tennis instruction booklet.

Without a doubt Vonnie Cassidy has the prettiest legs I ever saw, especially when she runs around her backhand. She's not really snooty either. She talks to people just fine. Except she uses words like *adore it* instead of *yeah* when I ask her if she can play tomorrow. Or when I buy her a Coke after, she'll say, "Thank you ever so much, Peter." It knocks me out. She also has this way she crosses her legs and hooks her foot on the back of her other ankle that kills me, and she has this little blonde fuzz on the top of her thigh. Good Lord, I'd like to kiss it. I can't believe myself. One day while we were sitting there waiting to get on the court she caught me staring at it—I know she did—and she asked, "Don't you find it terribly warm, Peter?" Then she looked off into the distance and brushed her hair back off her face with her fingertips. Like she was sitting on top of a mountain all by herself and had all the time in the world to kill. That's when I asked her to the Bonaventure High Sophomore Hop. She said okay and that I was so sweet to ask. My heart almost stopped.

I wish she could meet my grandmother, for some unknown reason. She'd probably think my family was nuts, though. Imagine Nard.

Mr. Cassidy eats dinner with his coat and tie on. You could have knocked me over with a feather. Mrs. Cassidy was all dolled up, too. In fact they were dressed fancier than we were. The soph hop was only dressy-sport, but her parents were dressy-dress and all they were doing after dinner was staying home and listening to *Fibber McGee and Molly*. In the conservatory, if you please. They were neat to have us all, though. And boy, are they polite. Everybody was, for that matter. Except Mary Frances Dennehy laughs with her mouth full. And Doc insisted on talking politics all through dinner. Sometimes I don't know about Doc. It was obvious Mr. Cassidy was more interested in the fact that Doc was driving us in his dad's broken-down '28 Hudson than he was in the Marshall Plan. No wonder. They have a new Packard. I just practiced being seen and not heard and tried not to snort. Harriet would have been thrilled. If you go to the movies at all and you know who Nick and Nora Charles are, the Cassidys are a lot like them, only Catholic. They call each other darling about a hundred times a night.

Vonnie had on this white angora sweater and a lime-green skirt and perfume. White Shoulders. By Lanvin. It's pronounced *Lah-vah*. Or something. It's French. She's also five-seven. God.

First we had tomato aspect, which I'd never heard of before and wanted seconds on, but nobody else did—so I'm glad I kept my mouth shut for once in my life. I did eat the lettuce underneath, though, which was wrong, I think. Mrs. Cassidy had this neat little bell by her plate, like the one at Mass, and every time she rang it this lady came out of the kitchen and served. They'd all smile at her, Vonnie too, and say, "Thank you so much, Sumiko," or "Delightful, Sumiko." Pretty hot stuff, if you ask me. Then we had the beef Stroganoff, which I did have seconds on. They even had little glass dishes for salt and pepper with tiny spoons in them. I couldn't believe it. For dessert we had chocolate moose. That's also a new one on me. And coffee.

That's when Doc finally got off the Taft-Hartley bill and decided to bore everybody about the UN, and I went out to lunch so to speak. I started having this day-dream about getting under the table—it's so embarrass-ing—and crawling up Vonnie's lime-green skirt. And licking her legs. I can't believe my own brain. I was just about at the licking part when Mrs. Cassidy rang the bell, either for more coffee or to shut Doc up. I don't know which, but it reminded me of *mea culpa* and I started to sweat. Holy Mother of God, what's going to become of me?

I don't want to talk about the soph hop for several rea-sons, sweat being only one of them.

I see my mom these days about twice a month, and I finally figured out a way to keep myself from getting sick on the Greyhound bus. One, you don't ever sit in the back row because you're right on top of the wheels. And two, you try to sit behind a lady with a hat on, and then you tear up little pieces of paper as small as you can and put them in her hat one by one. I know it sounds silly, but I haven't been bus-sick since I started. And just wait till she gets off at Seventh and Market and starts to walk through the bus depot with snow coming out of her hat. I get a big kick out of it.

I can just see myself telling Vonnie Cassidy that stupid story. I don't know about the art of conversation is the problem.

My mom and Ray (who practically lives with her) usually pick me up in his Cadillac, which you could eat off of. Even so, he gets a new one every two years, rain or shine. He makes a fortune at the races and wears a secret money belt. I'll bet they get married. He calls me son. My ambition in life is to stop Ray from feeling left out when my mom and I start yakking. And also to stop him from saying *nigger*. It's his favorite word when he talks about getting his car washed.

"Gee, Vonnie, what do you think about the Negro situation?" I can see me saying that, too. In a pig's ass. She probably never even talked to one. Besides, Doc's good at that stuff and I'm not.

At least Ray and I can talk about things. He almost had a head-on collision when I told him about the hat trick. My mom, too.

Harriet said *nigger* the other day when she was talking to Mrs. Mudge over the back fence about her husband's company picnic. She said they shouldn't be allowed to dance with white ladies. I was weeding at the time. All I said was they didn't like to be called that, and she asked me if I wanted a good slap across the face. Harriet, not Mrs. Mudge. Naturally, I said no, but I must've meant yes somewhere down deep because, stupid me, I also said I couldn't see what was so wrong about dancing with them. So I got my wish. She didn't hurt my feelings, though, because at the time I was thinking about my friend David Snowden who I'll probably never see again.

"Don't you glare at me, lunkhead." Three guesses who said that.

My dad stays at work late these days and sometimes he has a hangover in the morning.

You know who glares good? Burt Lancaster.

See, I can't do that. That's what I wish I could do with Vonnie. Just glare at her until she sinks into my arms. Instead I stepped on her feet all night, especially during "How High the Moon," and my stupid dick got in the way on the slow songs. Sometimes I wish I didn't even have a dick.

Once upon a time there was this beautiful girl who was very refined, and she fell madly in love with this boy with whom she went to a dance. They danced divinely together, and frequently everybody made a circle to watch them. When they weren't dancing, they sat out and talked about everything under the sun, and held hands. Her hands were extremely delicate. His were smooth and dry because he was very confident. He was so confident that even the fact that his wicked stepmother mother was a chaperon and that Jesus was also watching him like a hawk from the crucifix in the gym, he took no notice. He didn't even introduce his stepmother to the girl of his dreams. He just smiled bitterly at her on their way to the punch bowl. Needless to say, they danced cheek to cheek for "Goodnight Sweetheart," and he didn't even have to ask her if it was okay. She merely melted.

After the dance they went to the drive-in with their friends who talked about St. Thomas Aquinas all night, but our hero and his girl took no notice of that either. Instead, she fell limp into his arms, and he smelled her hair gently, and kissed her all over in the backseat, and she responded even though she was refined.

When he took her to the door, he definitely did not say may I. He glared at her. She looked up at him with green eyes and lips parted with desire. So he said, "Oh, what a rogue and peasant slave am I," and pulled her to him, giving her his best kiss. Soon, they plan to elope.

Peter Russo
1947

XIV ◆◆◆◆◆◆◆◆◆◆◆◆◆◆

I look pretty hot shit in my football uniform, if I do say so myself. The shoulder pads make you look like you've been doing Charles Atlas for about fifty years. We've got blue jerseys with gold numbers and white pants with blue helmets. Mine's too tight, but I don't mind because I don't get to play that often anyway, the main reason being I don't know beans about football. That's why they made me a tackle. The best players are the halfbacks and quarterbacks and ends, and of course John Spellman. People just naturally bounce off John Spellman, which is a good quality to have for a fullback. I bounced off him in practice the other day and got the wind knocked out of me. He was very understanding about it, though.

I don't think I have that burning desire Coach Crump is always barking at us about. Usually I have a burning desire for the game to be over, so I can get into the shower, where everybody says, "Good game, good game." That happened last week when the Bonaventure Bears creamed St. Elizabeth's, 33–13. John Spellman made three touchdowns, one of them right over left tackle, which was me at the time. *Over* is putting it mildly.

I couldn't help noticing his dick in the shower. I wish I could be John Spellman for just one weekend, or even borrow his dick, considering Bobbie Flaherty and God knows who else is bouncing off him on Saturday nights. There I go again. I wouldn't mind making a touchdown for once in my life either.

Father Lefty Cavanaugh is our assistant coach. Mainly he says Mass for the team on Saturday mornings before the game, and then he chain-smokes on the sidelines. He does it in twenty minutes, too. Mass I mean, which is some kind of a record. Fortunately or unfortunately, you can't understand a word of it. Meantime, we're kicking the crap out of everybody. So Mass is Mass, right? He's also the one who came over and talked my dad and Harriet into letting me play. By the time Father Lefty finished his second Manhattan, Harriet had him convinced she was the patron saint of San Mateo County and the next week she got elected president of the PTA. So who talked who. Figure it out.

I'd really like to squash her like a grape sometimes. Like when she runs her hand over the car after I've washed it and looks at me like I took a crap on it instead. Or when she grabs me by the ear in the basement after I've already swept it and she points at the corners. Or like I made this new friend Barry Hanson, for instance, who goes to San Mateo High, which is the public high school. He lives over on Quincy, but his dad drives a beer truck. Lucky Lager. So forget Barry.

We finally got a new car. Plymouth. Beige two-door. We kept the '36 Ford, though, which smells like an old Toscano by now, and I get to drive it when I get my license. My dad's giving me lessons on his days off and he makes me laugh so hard I get tears in my eyes. Instead of telling me to be careful, like an ordinary person, he says stuff like "It might be a good idea to miss that tree." I get hysterical. Once I almost hit a truck.

Next year I get to be a busboy.

Nowadays I have a newspaper route—186 papers. I go down to the *Times*, and we fold the papers into small squares, me and about fifteen other guys. It's called boxing. Then I load them on my bike and deliver. I also have to collect at the end of the month. If you want to be bored to death, try and get $1.20 from 186 people.

Ernie Holderegger is the best boxer. He and Kwan.

Kwan's squares look like Christmas packages, but Ernie's a hair faster. They're like these two blurs when they box. I box okay, but I'm not great.

And that's what I want to be. Great at something. John Spellman is great. Even old Doc is great, Mr. Straight-*A* and president of the debating society. My grades are passable, but I have to fix my *C*-minus in geometry to look like a *B*-plus till they sign my report card, and then change it back again for the simple reason I don't want to spend the next twenty years in my room trying to figure out the square of the hypoteneuse, which is what would happen if Harriet Einstein ever laid eyes on a *C*-minus. You need a very good ink eraser. Turns out I'm a great liar, which isn't exactly what I had in mind.

If you're great everybody looks up to you. It's as simple as that. I even made a novena to the Blessed Mother. Athlete was my first choice. I also said a Hail Mary or two for my pimples to go away. They come every Friday and dry up by Tuesday and then come back again on Friday. Wednesday and Thursday are my best days. I want my best days to be on the weekend, if that's not asking too much. I'm also making the Nine First Fridays. If you go to Mass and Communion every first Friday of the month for nine months in a row, you're guaranteed of getting into heaven. I've already made six. It's probably the only way I'm going to save my immortal soul considering the old monkey business,

which I'm convinced is how I got my pimples in the first
place. Spellman doesn't have one pimple. Meantime
Vonnie Cassidy said no when I asked her to go steady.
Naturally. Mr. Smooth. I said a rosary, but no dice.
Who cares?

My grandmother's a kick in the pants these days. She
got herself a cocker spaniel about three months ago.
Actually, she didn't get it. She's supposed to hate dogs.
We got it for her from the pound as a surprise, and
Nonna was so thrilled she almost hit my dad with a
frying pan. She's very fussy about her carpet, which you
used to be able to eat off of. I guess when the dog
started to sniff around the kitchen Nonna kind of melted.
So now it's Bonnie this and Bonnie that. She sleeps by
the stove and has buttered toast for breakfast and whatever she wants for lunch and dinner. Bonnie looks like
a basketball and also has shit for brains. She's crazy
about Harriet and scared of me. Which is how the conversation came up. Conversation is putting it mildly because as a rule my grandmother doesn't talk about love
stuff—unless it has to do with Nelson Eddy and Jeanette
MacDonald.

She was making soup when I got there, having just
completed my first solo drive outside of San Mateo. My
dad made me promise not to go over forty-five on the
bloody Bayshore (that's what they call it), which is a real
endurance test when you're driving a car that smells like

an ashtray and everybody else is whizzing past you at sixty. He wants me to take after him, I guess. It took me about a year to get to the city.

Anyway, I was having a snack and watching Nonna strain chicken and a lot of other stuff through a cloth. I'd go "Here, Bonnie, here, Bonnie," and the dumb son of a bitch would run under the stove and whimper. I even tried to give her a ravioli and I finally had to throw it at her. Nonna couldn't understand it. I think she was bent out of shape that anybody would actually run up to Harriet and try to jump in her lap. She didn't say anything, but I could tell. When Nonna gets really steamed up, she gets this expression that looks like she needs an Alka-Seltzer. Say when Clo gives her a recipe and leaves something out or when people don't finish their dinner.

All of a sudden she said "Goddamn it," which she never says, and threw a chicken foot into the sink. Then she dried her hands and grabbed me by the shoulders and said "I love you, Peter." Her eyes were wet. "There's nothing wrong with you just the way you are." How about that! Talk about feeling at home. She gave me a hug and almost crushed me to death. Then old Nard did this really funny thing. He's so nuts. He sort of acted out in pantomime that I should grab the dog and we'd put her tail under the rocker. And I said "Here, Bonnie," and Nard howled—and Nonna and I didn't know whether to laugh or cry.

◆ ◆ ◆

Wouldn't you know I wouldn't make the nine First Fridays on the first try. You'd think since Catholics are lucky enough to have First Fridays in the first place that I could at least be grateful and take advantage of it.

I don't have the guts to go to Confession at this particular time is the problem. No priest I ever went to would believe me anyway. They usually see me coming, Mr. Impure Thoughts. Ten Our Fathers and ten Hail Marys and that's all she wrote. I can just hear myself. "Bless me, Father, for I have sinned, Mrs. Brynjulson on 1513 Catalpa put my dick in her mouth." I'm sure.

The other problem is I'm not even sorry. Usually Mrs. Brynjulson just hands me a cookie or something for porching her paper and missing the roses, but this time she gave me a jelly doughnut and went into the other room to make change and when she came back with the $1.20, she was wearing this little green robe. So naturally, dumb me started getting a boner right away, even before she started talking about football and how muscular my legs probably were. Then I really got one. It didn't even matter that she was old. Forty probably. God. Or that she looked a little like ZaSu Pitts, if you go to the movies at all, who usually takes on the part of a nervous nitwit.

And get me. I didn't think I had it in me, never having done it in front of anybody before, but I couldn't get my pants off fast enough. "I'll bet you have big strong legs" is all she said, and dumb me said, "Would you like to see them?" I couldn't believe my own mouth. Naturally, she said yes. What was she going to say—no? She didn't even mind that I put the rest of my jelly doughnut on the piano. Harriet would have shit! I just yanked my Levi's off as fast as I could, having a little trouble getting them down over my, never mind, but I wound up just standing there wiping the sugar off my stupid mouth with this giant point in the middle of my shorts. What kills me is that I wasn't even embarrassed. My so-called big strong legs were shaking, but I wasn't embarrassed. I was running for a touchdown.

To make a long story short—actually it's a pretty short story as is—I just let her touch my legs as if it happens every day, except my head started to pound and I thought I was going to drop dead when she started kissing them, the thing I always wanted to do to Vonnie Cassidy and still do, only this time I was Vonnie Cassidy. When Mrs. Brynjulson finally pulled my shorts down and did it, I had to hold on to the piano. And then I went kerplunk in about one second. Talk about that's all she wrote. Turns out that's what I'm really sorry about. Not that I did it. That I went kerplunk in about a second. I can just hear myself. "Bless me, Father, I wanted it to go on forever."

I explained to Doc that I didn't have the chance to put my hand up her robe because she was kneeling down the whole time. That's when he told me that girls have three holes instead of two. I got a big kick out of that. I said you're full of crap because nobody has three holes unless they're in Ripley's *Believe It Or Not*, and what book did he ever get that out of? (He spends half his life in the library.)

Anyway, Mrs. Brynjulson canceled on me. I think she was embarrassed. I usually have a few extras, though, and now and then I just porch one for the hell of it.

XV ◆◆◆◆◆◆◆◆◆◆◆◆◆◆◆

My uncle Charley is such an asshole. He's had dinner at the Villa Paison about three times a week all summer long—and he always has a different girl with him, when he could probably have had Vivian Van Alden the whole time if he wasn't such an asshole. They're all really knockouts, too. They're always trying to hold his hand during dinner, which, if you know how Charley eats, isn't a good idea. I'll bet he makes out with all of them. You'd think Vivian Van Alden would be enough for anybody in his right mind. Imagine making out with Van Alden *and* all those other girls at the same time. Naturally, I don't mean at the same time. I mean the same week. Or month even. Imagine. So is he an asshole or isn't he? I mean, there's a good question.

I don't think he deserves it is the point. Besides, he acts like such a big shot. That's it. That's what makes him an asshole. Because he talks too loud and keeps his knife and fork in his fists all during dinner—I can just see him wolfing down Stroganoff with some people I know—and laughs at his own jokes. "What's cookin', Dom?" Yuk, yuk. That's supposed to be some hysterical comedy act when you walk into a restaurant looking like you just beat somebody up, which is exactly the way Charley walks all the time, come to think of it. And that's the main reason I didn't mind so much about the butter.

So last night I whispered to him on his way out of the men's room, "Please say hello to Vivian for me."

"She's getting married, kid." He smiled this asshole smile that said he didn't even care.

Which is reason number two I was almost glad I dropped the butter on his shoulder. Up his. I just decided to pretend I didn't notice. The truth is I also didn't have the guts to tell him because I'd already spilled a little minestrone in his lap—not very much— while I was getting a load of the headlights on Miss Fancy Pants. I don't even remember her name. *Tina.* Anyway, hotshot Charley walked out of the joint looking like a major general. I went into the men's and laughed my ass off.

The waiters at the Villa are a real kick in the head. Slow Motion, Flat Top, and Toots are my favorites. Except Flat Top got canned by my dad when he tried to show me how to carry this huge tray full of dirty dishes into the kitchen the fancy way with one hand above your head. It was like a Tom and Jerry cartoon. You couldn't see it from the dining room, but you could hear it in the next county just as he got into the kitchen. Boy, did he get yelled at. *"Non mi rompere coglioni, for chrissake!"* It means: don't bust my balls. And he was only trying to help. If my dad ever yelled at Harriet that loud, she'd shape up in about two minutes.

Slow Motion's a real character. He does this crazy thing every time he gets a tray of drinks from the bar. He jiggles it on his way to the dining room, and then after he serves it he heads for the kitchen and drinks the tray. It could be anything—beer, wine, Manhattans, martinis, whatever—down the hatch. He usually overtips me at the end of the night. Sometimes he forgets my name.

I guess I like Toots the best. He calls me handsome, and whenever I get a new pimple he shakes his finger in my face and smiles. Sometimes he pinches me on the butt, but it's all in fun. He overtips me, too. And is he smart! I like to have dinner with him at the end of the night. He should have been a teacher. He knows practically everything about literature and he's an actual descendant of Macbeth.

◆ ◆ ◆

So summer's over and we started out with *Macbeth* in English. Some coincidence. I liked it okay, but I like Lord Byron better. "Maid of Athens, ere we part, give, oh, give me back my heart!" He wrote that. Meantime, Snooty Vonnie Cassidy, Miss Too Busy to Go Steady or even play tennis lately, happens to be going steady with that prick John Spellman. How do you like them apples? And what's worse, she acts like she's so divinely glad to see me at dances. So does he. Like they're my parents or something. I feel like telling them to stick it, but I just smile like some asshole so he doesn't beat me up.

Plus, we stink in football this year, so I get to play first string. And thank God I finally found a helmet that fits. Recently, we got killed by St. Agnes, of all people, and last week even South City beat us 7–0, but it wasn't entirely my fault. I slipped is what I did because it was raining, so I didn't quite make my block. It wasn't as if I did it on purpose. Poor old Spellman really ate it. It was almost funny. Well, not funny exactly—there's nothing humorous about a sprained ankle. But when the Zambaca twins charged in over tackle—you should see them, Floyd and Lloyd, imagine having beards in high school, Floyd hit him high, I think it was Floyd, he has this scar, and Lloyd hit him low—you could hear poor old Spellman go "Oof, oof." Just before he fumbled and Lloyd jumped on it. I think it was Lloyd. Twin oofs.

That's what struck me so funny, I guess. I could've

gone all day without saying, "Nice tackle," I suppose, but I couldn't help myself. Besides it's good sportsmanship and it *was* a nice tackle.

I could see old Father Lefty jump up and down and slam his cigarette into a puddle just before he pulled up his cassock and waded in to help old Spellman off. Poor John. He kept going "Oof, oof" all the way to the sidelines. I had to look the other way. It's really no laughing matter, but you had to see the funny side, especially since Coach Crump pulled me out and pointed to the bench and told me I don't get mad enough. That's how much he knows.

Talk about eating it: we're also doing compositions this year—the point being I never saw Doc eat shit before. Not in class anyway. Usually it's me in trig. Doc eats it in the locker room after gym when everybody snaps towels at him, but *never* in class. It was pretty shocking. Wycoff read his composition out loud and practically accused Doc of being a fairy. Not that he said anything. It was the way he read the composition that was pretty unmistakable. With all kinds of pauses. It was a little flowery, I'll admit; but that's just Doc. He's very intellectual. "My Best Friend" was the title, and frankly I liked it a lot—especially the part about my hair and eyes. But I felt bad for Doc, naturally, because he's my best friend, too. Ironically, my composition was about *him*—what a brain he is and in spite of it how he's always losing his jacket. "The Absentminded Pro-

fessor." I was glad about my *A*-plus and that Wycoff
likes me, and sad about Doc's *C*-minus and that he got
laughed at. I hate it when I'm two things at once. Doc
says Wycoff's a cruel bastard and he'll never forgive
him.

I have no social life. I'm dating this Maureen Moran.
Primarily because I get too excited around popular girls.
(I don't even think about V.C. anymore. Up hers.) I
don't mean dating really. We don't go to movies on
Saturday night and hold hands or look at the moon, but
if there's a dance I'll ask her. She has brown hair. Her
best quality is she's pretty talkative. Her worst is she
kisses with her mouth completely closed. Even an ant
couldn't crawl in. She's best friends with Mary Frances
Dennehy, who passes out holy cards every five minutes.

I asked Doc, "How do you expect to get anywhere
with Mary Frances when she's practically married to
Jesus?" which is what they call it when you become a
nun.

"None of your business," he replied, but he was kidding. Then he got this little grin on his face and in-
formed me that Mary Frances was "a perfectly
acceptable relationship" because last summer he made
it all the way with a clerk at the Andrew-Williams store
in Palo Alto who was twenty and in college.

I said no! He said yeah. And I said so what was it
like, and he got very mysterious all of a sudden and

stuck his nose up and said quite good, quite good, and I said bullshit, and he said no bullshit, and I said I don't believe a word of it. But I do, because if there's anything Doc isn't, it's a liar.

Old Doc. He dropped the Charles Atlas course after about twenty minutes. Not much good it's doing me. The closest I get to a real make-out is to daydream about Vivian Van Alden at night. Or June Haver. Or Jean Simmons, who has an English accent and was in *Hamlet*, which I saw twice. "Get thee to a nunnery." Whoa, fat chance. Speaking of sexual education, Father Jumpy Houlihan gave us a lecture on it during religion the other day—because we're seniors and pretty soon we'll be going out into the world. He sort of looked at the wall and jangled the change in his pocket and said, "When you're married, if she wants it you gotta give it, and if you want it she's gotta give it." *Yeah, but what!!!???* Then he went back to the Immaculate Conception.

Barry Hanson's parents got him a backboard and a basket for his birthday. It's on their garage door. Sometimes I ask Harriet if it's okay with her if I go down to Fitzgerald Field and instead I go shoot baskets with Barry. I just hide my bike.

Barry's dad said I was welcome to come anytime I wanted. "Call me Steve," he said, which was pretty nice of him.

I call his mom Mrs. Hanson, even though she said, "Call me Mary." It's harder with somebody's mother. She makes a pot of coffee—cuppa joe, she calls it—after we shoot baskets, and she sits down and smokes a Herbert Tareyton and talks with us.

I don't know what possessed me, but last week I smoked a Herbert Tareyton right in front of Harriet. I did. After dinner. I was scared shitless. My dad was having a Toscano and I was having a Herbert Tareyton. Right in front of her. She went fruit. First I lit his and then I lit mine. Absolutely fruit. My dad was trying not to smile. She didn't hit, though. Just fruit.

"Oh, my, we're so adult now, smoking a cigarette. Who the hell do we think we are, big shot?"

I admit my eyes were glued to the table, but I kept puffing away as long as I could stand it without puking my veal sauté. I did it the next night, too. I'm getting so I can inhale a little. (Mrs. Hanson looks neat when she does it.)

Steve smokes cigars. Phillies. I told him what my dad smokes, and he said, "He must be quite a fella, your dad." I would imagine Steve is the best truck driver Lucky Lager has.

The senior ball was boring. We went to a dinner dance at the Fairmont Hotel. The Grand Ballroom. I had a tux on—it took me about three days to get the studs right.

Maureen wore some taffeta. It was turquoise, I think. It looked like two dresses. We had chicken with no bones in it—it's supposed to be ritzy—and peas. It was shitty. The only okay parts of the night were that old eagle eye was playing bridge with Mrs. Mudge instead of being a chaperon, as if I needed one, and Eddie Howard was appearing in the Venetian Room. It's only the most famous band in the country, so some of us snuck in. We heard him sing "To Each His Own."

By the way, Miss V.C. was decked out in this black strapless job with a pearl necklace and little earrings that matched. Doc said Mary Frances said it was real silk chiffon. Maureen said the pearls were real, too. Big deal. I smelled her a couple of times when she waltzed by with old Oof-oof. I could care less.

At about five the next morning—you're supposed to stay up all night—I also got the best kiss from the famous Maureen Moran that I'll ever get in my life. It happened in the backseat of Doc's broken-down Hudson. We were in the middle of this long-drawn-out kiss—which just about broke my teeth and put me to sleep at the same time if it hadn't been for the noise coming out of her nose—when all of a sudden she made this passionate growl, opened her mouth about a sixteenth of an inch, and buried her face in my lips. The trouble was I heard her lay this fart at the same time, right through her taffeta. I knew she was trying to cover the sound, but she was a little late. Some highlight. Pretty soon everybody sort of rolled down their windows at once. That was that. It was definitely a no-boner night.

I can't wait to go to college.

XVI ••••••••••••••••••

My bougainvillea is alive! The goner. The one I inherited in the divorce. I can't believe my eyes. The rains came and then the sun came, and now there's this tiny leaf the size of an imported pignoli (pignolo?) at the very top of a branch that looks like a sprig of dead parsley in the crook of an arthritic finger. "Ye Elements!" cried Lord Byron. "In whose ennobling stir I feel myself exalted . . ." One green leaf. Maybe half a shade lighter than my left hand, tinted, as it were, from stuffing and grinding my life away. Easy, boy.

Obviously, it's the Swiss chard. I crank with my right. What a nice storybook ending, though. I wonder if Jennifer would be pleased. The old boug lives. Should I call her or shouldn't I?

No. Over is over.

"Yo, Jen."

"Peter . . . ?"

"The same."

"I can't talk. I'm running bathwater."

See, there it is in a nutshell. First of all, it's the way she says *Peter* that knocks me out. British women have a knack for pronouncing those middle *t*'s that turns me to marmalade. La*t*er. Alliga*t*or. Can you hear it? The ordinary woman says Pe*d*er. Tall from Buckinghamshire says Pe*t*er with the tip of her randy little tongue making high-born contact somewhere around the front of her upper palate. I don't know where the hell it comes from. Julie Andrews is an expert. So is Audrey Hepburn. Ask them. And then she comes up with *bathwater*. The coup de grace. Bath as in bother, water as in Pee-teh. You can almost hear the chemistry:

Pee-teh, I cahn't talk, I'm running bahth waugh-teh.

Jesus Christ.

On top of this mixture break a dozen eggs.

Probably decked out in that shorty little robe, too, co-incidentally green, which I presented to her one summer evening along with a rose, no special occasion required.

(A dozen eggs seems like an awful lot to me.) Which, if memory serves me, she never removes until after she steps over and into the bahth. Truthfully, it's the old step-over and into that knocks me on my ass. *Ahss.* Sometimes I'd ask her, this is so silly, I'd ask her what are you doing, Jen honey, when it was perfectly clear she was getting ready to ease snakelike into the tub, but I'd ask anyway on the chance she might say *bahth* or *waugh-teh* or both. Even with impatience, that's okay, too. At the very moment of step-over. Then I'd bend down and pick up a piece of lint or something from the mat. God, the games people play.

"*Stop it, Peder!*" screeched my Olympia manual. "*Think of the hair in the drain!*"

She's so jealous it's pathetic.

> *Add four cups parmesan cheese.*
> *Add six packets imported pignoli.*

"Dad, what's the singular of pignoli?" The day my phone bill comes I run away from home.

"Of what?"

"*Pignoli.*"

"Pignoli . . . pignoli . . . pine nuts. I don't think there is one."

"I was just wondering for the hell of it."

"What?"

"*For the hell of it.*"

"The point being, you never use just one."

"Yeah, but wouldn't you think there'd be a singular? I mean, would you say 'I dropped a pignoli under the stove?' "

"Where?"

"Under the stove."

"Jesus, you got a point. Hang on a minute. Let me check my Italian dictionary. Where is that goddamn thing?"

"It's not important."

"The hell it's not. Now hang on a minute, I'm gonna put the phone down. Hang on." Seconds later, a small faraway voice: "Goddamn son of a bitch'n, here it is, no, that's, wait a minute, that's not it, goddamn it. . . ."

"Dad!"

"Aha! . . . *Aspetta* (hold your horses), *aspetta* . . . let's see. . . . Pine. Nut. Pacify . . . pack. . . ."

"Dad!"

"Package . . ."

"You're not wearing your glasses."

"The hell I'm not, and thereby hangs a tale. The goddamn things have acquired a habit for about a year now that annoys the hell out of me. If I look down, say, to read Herb Caen's column—oho, what a master, you should see this morning's—the fuckin' things drop down about . . . remember the little butter pats we used to use down the restaurant?"

"Uh-huh."

"About that size. The thickness of a butter pat. Quarter of an inch. And I wind up lookin' through the top part of what the hell do they call it . . . ?"

"Bifocals."

"Yeah, the goddamn bifocals, and I can't see a fuckin' thing!"

"It's the *frames*, Dad. When do you go to *Kaiser* again?"

"Oh, Christ, don't get me started on the superlative eye department at Kaiser Hospital," started Dom, thereby hanging another tale.

Apparently, everybody's a Chinaman. Apparently, none of them speak English. And that's apparently why Dominic hasn't had an eye examination or a frame touched by a foreign hand, or even cleaned his lenses in his own bathroom, for three years. For spite! The capper was when Dr. Fong, when asked by Dom if there was the possibiblity of a cataract in his future, made the fatal mistake of saying no cataracts, but he thought he saw a Ford. To which my father replied if he wanted Jimmy Durante, he'd turn on the fuckin' radio—whereupon he spun on his heel and walked blindly out the door, unassisted by his cane.

"Here it is, goddamn it!" he concluded. "Pine. Pina. *P-i-n-a*. Pina. Now. Nut. You got a minute?"

Soak the five slices of french bread in water . . .

(waugh-teh)

*till soft. Then squeeze dry and crumble it up into the
mixture. Then with your big mitts, mix, and I mean
mix. . . .*

I do have big mitts.

Yeah. I do.

Lusty mitts.

Broad-shouldered mitts. Macho . . . but gentle . . .

Caress my cahlves, tickle my thighs, kiss my ahss. . . .
So rang the telephone, ting-a-ling.

I knew it. Finished with our bahth, are we, all creamy
and cuddly in our teeny bikini, peek-a-boo fur akimbo?
Wishing, waiting, wanting? Missing the old creepie mou-
sie fingertips, the old feather touch?

"Answer the phone, Popeye!" Guess who from upstairs.

Okay, but I'm not about to take any crap.

"Don't be depressed, Peter," said a no-nonsense
voice from out the Marina.

"Mom?"

"Don't be depressed."

"I'm not."

"Mothers know these things, Peter."

"No, truly, I'm fine. I'm into the ravioli."

"God. Still?"

"The recipe's two typewritten pages, single-spaced."

"An opera, if I know your father. With him in the
lead. Honey, you'll get a kick out of this while I've got

you. I'm in the middle of the crossword and it says 'Robert blank of *The Untouchables.*' "

"Stack."

"Don't be such a smart-ass for a minute. The point is all I could think of was *Ness*. It took me till Thursday to arrive at *Stack*. So I said to myself it's easy to figure that one out, he's not my type. Never has been. Give me Burt Lancaster anytime. Boy, that Burt. You know who had that same quiet, well, let's call it what it is, honey: sex. You know who had it? Ray. Before he died."

"That's good, Mom."

"One touch, honey. Just one touch. Thrill is the word I want to use. I was a vegetable when I was married to your father, and Jesus, he was no help at all. Then I met Ray and I went for it like hogs for slop."

"I hear Herb Caen has a hell of an item in today's *Chronicle*."

"Honey, I've had Herb Caen up, down, and around. He's neither here nor there. Maybe the new San Franciscans like him. The immigrants. Which reminds me, I've been meaning to ask you for two times now. Do you ever hear from what's-her-name? Jennifer?"

"Never."

"Good. Now listen to me, honey. I know she had beautiful legs and a beautiful body and a pretty face. But, honey, who doesn't nowadays? They come along like streetcars. And she pushed you around, honey. You don't have to take that crap from anybody. Ray noticed it right away. He was something else, wasn't he? Ray? I mean, really, when you come to think of it. Never forget this, Peter, once a man gives a woman an orgasm, and honey, don't misunderstand me, Ray gave me plenty—a way of life, restaurants, a Cadillac—but once he gives her an orgasm, he keeps her for life, honey. For life."

Mix the whole thing till it becomes one unidentifiable mass.

XVII ·················

1. I hate my hair.
2. I hate my eyebrows.
3. I hate my lips.

And I don't know anybody. So much for San Mateo Junior College. They only have about a million girls, and everybody's in a damn club. Glee Club, Players Club, Flying Club, Forum Club, Bit and Spur. And good luck finding a Catholic. You really have to look. Which surprises me no end that I even care. But I wouldn't mind having something in common with somebody besides old tight lips Moran, Homemaking Club. These days she wants about ten kids. I see her in the cafeteria. Wait till she finds out what she has to do to make that dream come true. I just wave.

You know how you can tell who's popular? They roll their bobby socks. That's the system. It's very hot looking. The popular girls roll their bobby socks as far as they can below their ankles, and the unpopular girls don't. So which came first, the chicken or the egg? Who cares? It's a neat phenomenon and saves tons of time. The most popular chick on campus is Hilary St. James, this creamy blonde (Swim Club, Rally Commission, assemblies, homecoming, socials) who I'd make out with in a flash. Naturally, she doesn't know I exist, even though I sit right in front of her in biology. (Dr. Colby. The worst!) She crosses her legs every five minutes. I don't know how she keeps her socks from sliding all the way down into her shoes. Lately I've been reading up on syphilis and gonorrhea, and I wonder if it's all worth it.

I'd rather shoot baskets with Barry Hanson.

His dad got him a set of weights, too, so we fool around with them in our free time. Guess who got back into the habit of poking her bony finger into my chest every chance she gets. What the hell am I supposed to tell her. I'm down at Barry's body-building and turning queer, and I'm bringing all the Hansons home for dinner.

"You're doing *something* and I don't like it!"

"That's for me to know and you to find out!"

I didn't really say that.

4. I hate my personality.

For that very reason. Because I never say what I really mean unless it's yes to seconds on food. Mostly I make jokes. Also I see all the girls naked. Don't I wish. I mean in my mind's eye, if she's got her socks rolled down. And that's no joke. I see her ankles first, and then I work my way up. Sometimes I work my way down, but not too often. Mostly up, unless she's walking by me fast, and I wouldn't blame her, in which case I see her all at once. Like a snapshot. I wish they'd make special glasses. And then if I have to stop her and ask for directions (the campus is very spread out) I know she knows she's naked, like in some special room in my brain, so I look down at my big feet. "Hi, my name is Peter and I'm sorry." God. Then I force myself to think about the clap, which is also no joke. And get this! If she doesn't bother to roll her socks down, then I'm terrific. I pretend I'm popular. I horse around. Strange is what I am.

I'm not exactly Mr. Normal with the guys either. Like if I don't say something hilarious right away, they're going to yawn or something.

Meantime I'm boring the crap out of myself.

1. I *don't* hate gym. Mr. Hatzenpiller.

2. I *don't* hate Journalism 1-A. Mr. Birdwell. I better not. It's my major.

3. I *don't* hate Play Reading 103. Miss Shaw, who

every guy in class would like to boff if you could take a poll, because she's got neat knockers and this English accent. Christ, don't get me started.

Among the motley group of bewildered freshmen, possessing that chronic half-anxious, half-worried demeanor, are six notables. I wrote that. My very first article for the school paper. *The San Matean.* The first notables I mentioned were two shortstops and a quarterback, and then I went on to say *Included in the overwhelming influx of young women who grace the campus are pert Ann Peters, brisk Barbara Buckley, and lanky Laura Chessman.* Three girls I don't have the guts to talk to.

I finally wised up and decided to shave between my eyebrows. Toots suggested it Saturday night after everything quieted down in the dining room and we were having dinner. Capretto. It's goat. Baby goat. It sounds funny, but it's delicious if you think about something else. Think about lamb. Actually, Toots suggested plucking them, but forget it. Nobody believes this, but my grandmother prefers the capretto head. Imagine her eating a head. It's supposed to be some big Italian delicacy. Every time we get capretto in the restaurant, which isn't very often, Nonna always yells at my dad, "Bring me a head, bring me a head!" You can hear her three feet away from the phone. Anyway, it's funny how one thing makes you think of another.

So Toots said there wasn't anything fundamentally

wrong with my hair either—nothing that a little imagination wouldn't cure. Simply ask my barber to leave a tad more on the sides, that's all, to sort of frame my face. I love the way he talks. A tad more. Frame my face.

Toots knows so much about so many things it's incredible. Like about when the Roman army invaded Scotland (80 A.D.) and then something about the emperor Hadrian. I didn't get every detail. Anyway, everybody intermarried and the Picts were eventually converted to Christianity, and since Toots was related by marriage to Malcolm who was Macbeth's son, there was an excellent chance he was also a direct descendant of Jesus Christ Almighty. I almost fell into my capretto. About his two-thousandth cousin, I guess. Toots seemed pretty convinced, but I don't know. He also told me to stop worrying about my lips, for goodness' sake, that they were just fine and I didn't have anything to worry about on that score.

You know who'd like Toots?

Doc.

I can see them debating the Holy Roman Empire or the existence of God or something. That's pretty much how Doc got his scholarship to Santa Clara. His debating skill, plus the longest essay ever written: "Proof of the Existence of God." I read it. Part of it. Jesus. As far as I'm concerned, you either have the faith or you don't. It's that simple. He's taking epistemology, for God's sake. I don't even know what it means. Logic, I think. I missed Mass twice this month.

It was really strange the first time it happened. I was driving down Borel Road on my way to St. Matthew's, and I was a little late, so there was a chance I was going to miss the Gospel anyway, which if you do, you might as well stay home because you've missed Mass altogether. That's just the way it works. So I whipped down Quincy and had a cuppa joe with Barry and Steve and Mary. The second time I got invited for breakfast. Sausage and eggs. Timed it perfectly, too, so when I got home it looked like I'd been to ten o'clock Mass.

"How was Mass?"

"I didn't go to Mass, dipshit!"

What I really said was *fine*.

Unlike Doc, Barry isn't very talkative, but he sort of gives you the impression he's sincere. For instance— this is a dumb example—when he said "How do you like your eggs?" It's not exactly an earthshaking question, but when a guy looks you right in the eye and puts his hand on your shoulder, no matter what he says, it makes you want to jump up and down and yell or something. I don't know what the hell I'm talking about. He's also got the shiniest loafers I ever saw. That's Barry's best quality, next to the fact that his triceps are better than mine.

See, there. I'm doing it. That's supposed to be a joke, ho, ho, ho, and I'm doing that a lot lately. Especially in the cafeteria. It's huge. With a jukebox. A-12: "Dear One" by Les Paul and Mary Ford. Mary Chevrolet. Yuk, yuk. See what I mean?

I'm a card. I should be shuffled and dealt with.

BULLDOGS BEAT LOOP LEADING LOBOS.

That's the first thing I ever wrote for the sports page. It's a headline.

That Ray is something else. He and my mom got married. Finally. No big wedding, they went to Reno for a week.

RAY REARDON ROPES
RELUCTANT ROSIE RUSSO.

Don't ever call her Rosie. And don't ever call him late for dinner. Last night my mom made this wicked beef stew, and after she served it, Ray stared into my plate—he always does, to make sure we have exactly the same amount of gravy and I don't have one more little chunk of meat than he does. If I do, I eat it fast, while he's ordering another Jack Daniel's. Boy, is she attentive. Also, you have to keep reminding Ray that he's included in the conversation, even though he refuses to get a word in edgewise. And you know what else he does? He vacuums under the table after we finish dinner. Even though, if you know my mom, she already did it before I got there and she'll probably do it again in the morning. This way he'll sleep, honey, she says. I think they're going to be really happy together.

Anyway, last night he was feeling a little left out. You can tell: he plays with his food. So I decided to try it. I put my hand on his shoulder and looked him right in the eye and said (he belongs to this club; who doesn't?), "Ray, explain to me again why they exclude Negroes from the Masons." It worked. He felt included.

I love the custard pie in the caf. Seconds and thirds. I'm becoming notorious.

XVIII ⬩⬩⬩⬩⬩⬩⬩⬩⬩⬩⬩⬩⬩⬩

"Mother Nature has a way of putting a look in someone's eyes, and the owner hasn't a goddamned thing to
do with it." My dad said that over a beer.

Funny, he never mentions anything about Harriet
when we're alone. Naturally, I pretend she doesn't exist
every chance I get. Maybe he does, too. I don't know.
I'm chicken to ask. I've been working my ass off this
summer. I smell like everything on the menu. And I
don't have the energy to do much of anything after we
close up, except have a quiet beer with my old man.
He'd kill me if he heard me say that. Actually, he's not
old, he's just tired. We have this ritual after he does the

books and everything balances on the adding machine tape. He loves to see those double zeroes, it's from working in the bank. "Monkey nuts," he says, and we flop at the bar, hang loose, light up, and pop a couple of brews. Fatherly Advice 101. I like it. How not to be a marmeluke.

I can't believe he said what he eventually said. First we went through the usual palaver. Keep your grades up. Keep your ass out of the Korean War. For chrissake, don't get too serious with girls. There's only a one letter's difference between a champ and a chump. Then he took a big swig of his Bud. I love to watch his Adam's apple go up and down.

"Women come along like streetcars," he said.

What a crock.

I didn't say anything because I didn't want to get hit with a bottle (joke), but when you think about it, why the hell didn't he transfer from the one he's been on for twelve years. So I took a swig of Lucky Lager. "How did you meet my mom?" I said instead, getting ready to duck, because I'm supposed to call her Rose around the house so what's-her-name won't get offended.

He told me he noticed her legs first. How about that for a coincidence? And then he asked her to dance. Garibaldi Hall, south side of Broadway between Kearny and Montgomery, 1920.

"Is it still there?"

"Hell, yes."

"Do they still call it Garibaldi Hall?"

"I sure as hell do."

"One, two, three, dip?" I asked him, trying to picture it.

"Christ, no. Your mother and I wouldn't be caught dead doing a dip." Charleston, one-step, fox-trot. That was their style apparently, and all night long. He chugged his beer. "You know, Mother Nature has a way of putting a look in someone's eyes, and the owner hasn't a goddamned thing to do with it."

Naturally I heard him, but I wanted to hear it again. "What?" I said.

"You heard me. *Fa presto!* Finish your beer and let's get the hell outta here."

It was in the Jaycee parking lot that I told Alice Hochman I loved her. But I don't. I like her. I like Alice a lot. If I had my druthers, of anybody in the world to fall in love with, it'd probably be Joan Fontaine. But Alice said it first—while I had my hand down her panties in the Chrysler during lunch. So I felt kind of stuck and I just said I love you back. What was I supposed to say? It seems almost impolite to just go uh-huh or something equally benign when it's pouring rain and the windows are all steamed up and you're playing with each other in her dad's car. Don't misunderstand me. She's attractive, not whistle bait (Mother Nature put gloom in her little brown eyes), but pretty, except for her hips—and let's face it: I'm not exactly Burt Lancaster.

Hochman is pronounced Hook-man. Her dad says Hoockhckhckhman. Like radio static. I just call her the Hook, for short—not to her face, and not disrespectfully either, but it really cracks Barry up.

Harriet kills me. She insists that I date for one reason and one reason only, and that's all I ever think about. I hear that every weekend.

"And don't tell me otherwise!"

"*Aw, take a Miltown!*"

Not really.

She's right, in a way. But she's wrong in a way, too, because truthfully, although I love putting my hand there, what I like best about the Hook is that she's a nonconformist. I practically got on my knees and begged her to roll her socks down. On several occasions. But no. "I'm somewhat of a nonconformist, Peter, is that okay?" Sure it's okay, I never even heard the word before, much less met one. I just avoid the ankles, that's all. She also knows a ton of stuff about ballet and painting. And, I might add, she cleared up a few misconceptions I had about nookie in general. I still wish she'd do her socks.

How I met Alice was in the cafeteria. She stopped by one day and told me how much she enjoyed my weekly column in *The San Matean*. "The Trash Can," by Peter Russo. She said she was amazed we hadn't gotten acquainted last year. Turns out we've been in biology together for a century along with Hilary St. James. Well, there's your answer. Miss Hot Legs Hilary, who I took naked pictures of all the while I was dissecting my stupid frog. You're supposed to get his brain out in one piece, forget it, Cream of Wheat, and who gives me lover's nuts at Swim Club every Wednesday. So Alice sort of waddled up to me and said, "Hi, I'm Alice Hochman and I think you're a riot."

THE TRASH CAN
by Peter Russo

I've got more troubles than a nearsighted umpire with the seven-year itch! This humor column was supposed to be handed in yesterday. Instead it's going in tomorrow. I've been busy as a one-eyed peeping Tom and I can't think of a thing to write about. Also, today was the unluckiest day of my life. I drive to school in a car that hasn't got the power to blow the steam off a cuppa joe. I feel like a test pilot in a yo-yo factory. I show up at the cafeteria, and getting served is like trying to catch fish by beating the water with a broom. On top of that, there's no custard pie. Looking over at the next table, I spy a girl with knee action that'd make a Nash jealous. I look at her like a vulture with an option on a massacre. She turns away. I straighten out like a wet wash in a dry wind and see more red than the bleachers at a bullfight. . . .

It goes on. Anyway, the Hook and I had coffee and one thing led to another, so I guess we're going steady.

You know who quit? Toots. I couldn't believe it. Personal reasons, he said. That's all he said to my dad. Personal reasons. So? What are you going to do? They'll probably hire some asshole to replace him. We shook hands at the end of the night and said goodbye. It's going to be dull as hell without him. He even got a little flushed when we shook hands. Imagine a forty-year-old bald-headed guy getting flushed. I know the feeling. "We had some good talks, didn't we?" That's what he said to me when he left. I know he thought I was special. I'm not stupid. But I don't care. Toots has about six names, wouldn't you know it, but his last two are MacGreggor Gregg.

I get flushed at the Swim Club every Wednesday between four and five. In fact, I'm surprised I haven't had a heart attack and drowned.

OVERSEXED STUDENT SINKS
ONE-TRACK MIND CITED

It doesn't even rhyme.

For the first couple of weeks all I could do was swim two fast laps to make it look natural, then glom on to the side of the pool and stare at her like some lunkhead.

She's usually yakking it up with six clowns over by the candy machine. I finally worked up enough courage to ask her one day, "Hey, what's the difference between Dr. Colby and his ugliest frog?"

"I don't know," she said. "What?"

"Webbed feet," I said.

So, it's a tad corny, but it got old Hilary to sashay over to the edge of the pool. She wears this bathing suit. Heart attack number one. A two-piece job, blue with a red and white stripe on each side. And the bottoms are like these very short trunks.

So?

Who wouldn't?

Every Wednesday. Like clockwork. Two laps, hit the edge and hug it, while she stands there with her hands on her hips and her leg bent, and we talk biology. It's going to kill me. Then I have to swim around like some fanatic and force myself to worry about my grades or something so I can limp out of the water looking like a halfway decent human being while St. James sashays back to the candy machine.

It's blonde. Honey blonde.

The Hook's is black.

Which is okay, too. The trouble with the Hook, if the truth be known, is that she doesn't know how to do stuff right. Miss Two Fingers, instead of her whole hand. And too hard. *Exactly* like a hook. Not that it doesn't work. It works. But what am I supposed to say to her? Pretend your hand is this big feather? I'm not about to stop right in the middle of the proceedings and explain precisely what I mean. She's always looking for meanings. Like *life*. Screw it. It's okay the way it is. It's fine.

Barry Hanson is joining the navy.

I was shocked.

He announced it over one of our regular Sunday breakfasts. I said, "You're kidding."

He said, "Nope." A regular Gary Cooper.

I said, "What about the war?"

He said, "Far as I can tell, it's not a navy war."

I said, "What about school?"

He said, "I tell ya, Pete. I just don't know what the hell I want to do with my life, and I need some time to think it over."

I said, "Wow."

XIX

What she did was spread all my weight-lifting magazines onto my bed. I'd had them for over a year, since Barry and I started collecting them. She knew just what drawer to go into. She's very neat, so none of the magazines were touching one another and all the covers were facing up. Like a new bedspread. Roy Hilligen was in the middle, Mr. America 1951. Her lecture for the day, if not the entire course, was scrawled in lipstick on the mirror over my brown dresser. Motherhood 1-A, Harriet Russo presiding: I THINK YOU'RE A QUEER!

I'd just gotten home from Swim Club, so I was already bushed, but Harriet's rearrangement made me feel sick to my stomach and weak in the knees. Some combination. But not confused for a change. Not at all. Pretty clear-headed, actually. As if she'd vacuumed the corners of my brain, and the least I could do was acknowledge her.

"Harriet?"

"*What?*"

"Can you come in here for a second, please?"

"*What!*"

"Fuck you."

Well. You can imagine.

She snarled, she growled, she punched. I caught one wrist midair. She'd telegraphed a right to the head, her favorite. I caught the other one on its way to becoming a left to the chest, and I squeezed. Each one. Like a grape. And I glared at her, really glared, till everything grew very quiet and we looked like a couple of statues. I could hear Mrs. Mudge watering her lawn.

"Just wait till your father gets home," she said finally. Almost serenely. For her, anyway.

What a crock.

I'm squeezing your wrists so hard—if this was a cartoon your hands would've popped up through the ceiling by now. And you're talking to me like I forgot to clean the baseboards. You're a little scared, almost pretty.

So I released her. I nearly put a hand on her shoulder to include her even further, but I didn't want to press my luck.

"Fuck you, Harriet." In the Name of the Father and of the Son and of the Holy Ghost.

Amen.

Boot camp is the shits.

I've come to the conclusion that I hate all new places. But I don't think I'm going to get used to this one. It's in San Diego, and it gets too hot and too cold and all you do is march everywhere—and you should see what the United States Navy did to my hair. So much for framing my face.

So much for ever eating a decent meal again, for that matter. I had my last good dinner the night before all the new recruits had to meet at the YMCA in San Francisco—just before we boarded the train and some little creep invited me to share his peanut butter sandwich in the john. It's a whole new world out there.

The dinner was at my grandmother's. I brought Alice. Nonna was trying not to cry, Clo was sobbing, and Nard was Nard. When I introduced Alice—she's very quiet around new people, so she sort of looked at her shoes—Nard yelled, *"She's ashamed!"* at the top of his voice. He meant shy, but it sure shut her down for the rest of the night. Poor Nard spent the whole evening saluting me, rock, rock, rock, and laughing his ass off, and my dad spent it trying to make everybody else feel jolly. The ravioli was perfect, but guess who was pissed off. Big surprise. And you know why she was pissed off? She'd assumed—and this is how smart she is—that I'd be going into the navy as the captain of the ship.

"You're *not* going to be an officer?"

"No, I'm not." Straight. Right in the old eyeball.

Can you hear it? "Allow me to introduce my wonderful son, Rear Admiral Russo." She sulked for a week. She was also pissed off that Nonna and Clo took it so hard that I was leaving, which eventually pissed off Nonna and Clo, and made my dad do double duty and pull out some hysterical tales he remembered from the old days at the bank—stories we'd all heard twenty times.

You know who wasn't a wreck?

Me.

Now I'm a wreck.

You don't even have time to think here. You live with eighty guys, half of them from the South and the other half from South Fillmore Street, and they hassle over the Civil War every night of the week. I get such a headache. I even went to sick bay one night. That's what they call it: sick bay. But they just handed me some pills, APCs, All Purpose Cure, and sent me right back to wonderful Company 128 so I could enjoy breakfast with my shipmates. Shit on a shingle.

As it turns out, the guys that aren't hassling are crying in their bunks because they miss their moms. I don't miss anybody.

You know who I miss? The Nonconformist. You don't find many of those in the barracks. We decided it was for the best not to wait four years for each other. In my yearbook she wrote, "These hands of man, where to, what next? All my love, Alice." Good question. It's from Carl Sandburg. Old Hilary wrote, "Remember Biology!" How're you supposed to jerk off with eighty guys in the same room? At least, thanks to the Hook, I know the difference between a Gauguin and a Utrillo. I can't wait to share that piece of information with Billy Ray Berschwanger, who sleeps on top of me.

Harriet dropped dead. Yesterday.

He'd just finished washing the Plymouth and she bent down to scrape a speck off the hubcap with her fingernail and she never got up again. Heart, my dad said.

I tried to concentrate on something else. Anything. The cruddy bed, the cruddy dresser, the cigar box where Camille stuck my ten bucks. At least that's what she said her name was. "Hi, I'm Camille. Take your clothes off, sweetie." Meantime she's standing there in the nude washing my dick with warm soapy water, telling me what a beaut it is. I didn't know they did that. And all I can see is her face. Not Camille's. *Hers.* Old eagle eye staring up at me from the casket with her eyes closed, I know that doesn't make sense, with too much makeup on and mad as hell. Kerplunk. Right in the goddamn basin.

"It's okay, Peter, cry." Everybody kept saying that. "Cry, cry." As if I had a lump in my throat. Mostly Mrs. Mudge and the Bonaventure PTA ladies. I even tried biting my tongue, hard too, but no dice. God, I hate the smell of gardenias. Finally I made my face look like it was having a good cry just to make everybody happy. My dad shed a few tears. She was dressed in his favorite outfit, gray with stripes, but he didn't exactly throw himself into the coffin either. Nonna was at the dentist.

And I get horny.

At the mortuary.

I mean, really, Peter.

Here's Father Lefty whipping out this entire rosary, the Sorrowful Mysteries, at a non-Catholic funeral yet, very rare, and I'm mumbling "Holy Mary, Mother of God" and making big plans to get laid. And I'm not even looking at anybody's legs or anything. I'm looking at her! Paying attention for once in my life. If she could just see me now. Everybody's whispering how nice I look in my uniform.

Figure that one out.

There's this little town. Watsonville. The primary topic of conversation among all the waiters at the Villa, with the possible exception of Toots. And this particular ho-tel, which shall remain nameless, and whose directions

I just happened to have on the back of an old student-body card. It only took me two whole hours out of my life to drive down there. And for what? Plus I consumed about a pack of Beechnut gum. Who needs bad breath? Try it sometime on a sore tongue. And when I finally found the place, not exactly your Mark Hopkins, it took me another half hour to walk around the block to get the guts to ring the doorbell.

You know how long it took me to take my clothes off?

Forever.

My shoes. My goddamn shoes. My legs were shaking so bad, I used this chair—brilliant—and I kept hitting myself on the chin with my own knee. That's so like me.

"Straight or half and half, honey?"

She was pretty, too. No Joan Fontaine, but five-foot-two-eyes-of-blue and a crooked smile. My very first naked woman, standing there with a bar of soap in one hand and a washbasin in the other. It was brown. Light brown.

"Half and half would be fine." Whatever that is. I sort of knew.

God, what if there's a fire?

I tried to concentrate, I really did: the pictures on the wall, President Truman, Breathtaking Yosemite Valley. Forget it.

"Oooooh, who do you play football for?"

"Notre Dame."
Kerplunk.

So where to? What next?

A sub chaser probably, in the middle of the Pacific in the thick of it, and never write another word as long as I live. Never get laid either.

XX

"**W**hat are you doing, Peter?"

Maryanne starts every conversation with an accusation.

"You know very well what I'm doing."

"It's been three fucking days, Peter." This time she sang it.

"Creating ravioli is like creating an opera, Maryanne. One doesn't just slap it together. There's music, staging, characterization. . . ."

"*Faust* clocks in at under three hours, Petey. The whole thing is obviously too forensic for words. Why don't you just jump into that mass of dago chow and cuddle up and rub it all over your . . ."

"I made a plan and I'm finishing it!"

"Uh-huh. And then what are you going to do with your life, cherries jubilee?"

". . . . ."

"Peter?"

"Yeah."

"Well?"

"What you don't understand is that I prefer not to push the river, to remain in the now, so to speak."

"In the now, my ass," yelled the genius from upstairs.

"In the now, my ass." Maryanne cackled. "Aren't you this jerk who makes a list for everything? Wake up, go to the john . . ."

"Not really, no."

"You are, you do, face it, Peter. You've got the brain of a soufflé, a puff of wind, and on top of it you're a fucking wuss." The problem is I tell her everything. "Do I know my Petey, or don't I?" Cackle, cackle, cackle.

"Don't you have work to do?"

"Now, listen to me, grab a pencil, I want you to put this on top of your stupid list. One, hang up the phone. Two, write a page of something. Now, anything, one fucking page. I don't give a shit if it's on the back of a shopping bag. Push the river, Petey."

Gelson's Market, aisle twelve, exotic pasta. A chance meeting of shopping baskets. Click.

"Excuse me."

"Excuse me."

We chatted briefly over rigatoni, ditalini, capellini, presently segueing through things al dente to exotics in general as we stood, shoulders barely touching at the checkout counter, eyes locked in the now. She'd adore a cup of coffee, she said, and I said so would I, and together we said your place or mine, and shared a good laugh over an old cliché.

How deftly the world can reduce itself and nestle in the crook of a finger passing the sugar . . .

"Crap!"

"What?"

"You heard me."

"Mind your own business up there. It's not easy writing on a shopping bag. Besides. It's *my* fantasy."

"Crap, crap, crap."

Notice how she always has to have the last word.

"Olympia! From Mount Olympus I suppose!"

Wiseass. I yearn for the exotic, that's all. The chance meeting if you will. For instance, I met crazy Jennifer under the table at a costume party. How 'bout them apples. She was a Sister of the Holy Cross, too. With a slit up her habit. Where do you go from there? You tell me.

Back into the woods is where you go. To recapture.

God.

Old Jen.

I had a Christmas tree one year that was bent in the middle because I shopped late, and I'll be damned if I didn't fall head over heels for it, too. Hated like hell to see it go after the holidays, I might add.

I don't get out enough, period, is the problem. Know where I had my last chance meeting? In the dentist chair with spit on my face. Judith Steinmetz, D.D.S. Inc. Forget it.

"Scrape, scrape, scrape."

"Gnnghgnng."

"Mah heavens!" She was from Abilene.

"Gnngh?"

"A fahve-millimetah pocket on numbah fo-wer bah-cuspid, mah heavens!"

"Gng!" I'm such a sucker for an accent.

Oh, sure she was gorgeous. Christ, they all are. Eyes like walnuts about six inches from my face, peppermint breath, and all those fingers in my mouth. I just lost it, I guess. So we went to a Woody Allen movie, and I had to explain it to her over a cheeseburger for about six weeks.

> . . . *moving the world at will with my lips, slowly toward her places, listening a lover's listen for a catch in her sigh that told me secrets. . . .*

"Ah have asked you. Do *not* put your mouth down there."

"Just for a second. Pretty please?"

"Ah don't like it."

"But you've never tried it."

"Ah still don't like it."

And forget the games people play.

"Be who? Vanessa Redgrave? I cain't do that."

"Then I'll be Paul Newman, for chrissake."

"Ah cain't do that either."

If the consistency of the mixture is too dry, add more eggs. If it's too wet, add more cheese.

It's fine. I'm never going shopping again.

Then mix again thoroughly.

Not on your life.

Then put a lid on it, and let's talk about pasta.

Let's.

Pick up two four-foot sheets of dough from a ravioli factory.

?

Also a three-foot rolling pin, a three-foot roller-shaper with one-inch square compartments a quarter of an inch apart, and a cutter. Simply spread the filling an inch and a half thick onto the bottom sheet, then cover it with the second sheet. But don't cover the bottom sheet entirely. Leave a one-inch empty border all around so that too much filling doesn't squish out onto the floor.

Aw, for chrissake.

And for chrissake don't forget to flour the table (the bigger the better) first. Or,

Give up opera altogether.

even easier, use wonton.

Wonton?

"Saved by the Chinese?"

"Christ, yes, how do you think pasta arrived in Italy in the first place?"

"Gary Cooper."

"Marco Polo, you're goddamn right. You got a pencil handy, you might want to write this down."

"I'll try and keep it in my head."

"Huh?"

"I'll memorize it."

"Don't be a marmeluke, make a list."

"Shoot."

"One, place half a tablespoon of filling on a three-and-a-half-inch-by-three-and-a-half-inch wonton. Two, moisten the edges. Very important step. Three, place another wonton, same size, over the top and squeeze the edges."

"Yeah, but that just makes one ravioli."

"Right. What's the rush? Which reminds me, by the by, apropos of our earlier conversation about pignoli, I can't put this goddamn dictionary down . . . where is

that son of a bitch . . . ah . . . just in case you think
your old man is slipping, listen to this. 'Ravioli . . . often
used term to describe the singular.' Who ever heard of
one raviolo? *Capisce*?"

XXI

U.S.S. JONATHAN J. BAKER, APA 32
Yokosuka Bay

PLAN OF THE DAY:

0600 - REVEILLE.

0700 - MORNING MEAL.

0745 - QUARTERS FOR MUSTER.

0800 - TURN TO.

1200 - NOON MEAL.

1300 - TURN TO.

1600 - LIBERTY.

1630 - EVENING MEAL.

1815 - MOVIE CALL.

2200 - TAPS.

I wrote that. Pretty snazzy, huh? I get to do it every day, providing it doesn't interfere with my filing. Yeoman First Class Donny Lee Shirk gave me a shot at the job several months ago and he kind of liked my style. I also get to type it on an A. B. Dick stencil, run it off on the mimeograph machine, and distribute it to every bulletin board on the ship, which is 491 feet long, 65½ feet wide, displaces 8,889 tons of water, and has a draft of 25 feet 8 inches from waterline to keel.

I don't even know if we have a keel. Show me. We haven't moved in eight months. I'm prone to exaggeration. We creak. We've also got a ship's complement of thirty-five officers and 523 assholes who insist on giving you their life story on the toilet.

I drink too much.

I mess around a little, too. Lately. A lot. For some time now. It only costs a dollar and a half.

"Excuse me. Bartender? *Dokoni toire ga arimasuka, dozo?* Just in case I have to go to the toilet. Okay? And may I have another beer please? *Dozo.* I am sorry I do not speak your language, but you have a very pretty country here. *Yokosuka.* Very nice place. Rest assured. My pleasure. *Domo arigato.* Listen. Listen. Know who that is? Goddamn Kay Starr. *The wheeeeel of for-hor-tune . . . goes spi-hin-ning a-round.* Sorry. Neat though, huh? If I get the clap, I'll kill myself. Wanna hear a secret? We're shippin' out of this shithole next week. How do I know? Debbie-san told me so. That's how come I know that little piece of factual information. The point is the clap is a very big item on the *J. J. Baker* is the point. Know what I hate? When old Debbie-san or Suzie-san or whoever-san hits the mat with her socks on and keeps tellin' me what she's not gonna to do to me. I hate that. 'Suck-a-hachi *nevah hoppen*, Joe.' First of all, my name is not Joe. My name is Peter-san. *Not* Peterson. Peter-*san*. How d'you do? We got a Peterson, though, but he's not me. Actually, we got a couple of 'em. Three, I think. And second of all, forget suck-a-hachi. How 'bout a little conversation-hachi? *Capisce*? Like maybe where you went to school, or like about what's *gonna* hoppen, never mind what's *not* gonna hoppen. You believe in heaven? I dunno either. My grandmother sent me this big box of Italian salami before she died. I still got a chunk in my locker—it lasts forever. I'm goin' to the head, don't steal my beer. . . . "I can't go when somebody else's in the room. Sorry 'bout that. No shit, I can't even take a piss 'less I pretend I'm in the Russian River. Know what I hate? When your legs fall asleep. One cannot, however, get the clap from a toilet seat, I am told. One does not have to stick it in all the way either, I am told. Jus' a lil bit. *The wheeeeeeeeel of forrr-horrr-tune* . . . Am I disturbing anyone? A thousand pardons. *Non mi rompere coglioni*, for chrissake. . . ."

♦ ♦ ♦

Aloha from Waikiki.

Gippy takes her fencing lesson on Wednesday nights, so I'm home alone.

Lounging.

Is that a great name? Gippy. With a *j* sound, obviously. And I'd be willing to bet nobody in my family ever took a fencing lesson, even if you went all the way back to Italy and looked it up.

Lounging in my lava-lava. Which is a male sarong. Most people don't know that. Sipping a snifter of Rémy Martin. It's cognac and a snifter is what you drink it out of, obviously. Actually, you sip it. Listening to a little Brubeck, "Jazz Goes to College," our favorite. Checking my reading list. Let's see . . . *The Little Prince*, Philip Wylie, Henry Miller, never mind, and marveling, I guess you could say, at a three-foot oil impression of Isabel Han experiencing a self-induced orgasm, I'm learning a lot these days, on which Gippy's putting the finishing touches, touché, using only memory and a palette knife.

Gippy yanked me from the lobby of the Moana Hotel "by the scruff, eons ago," I love the way she exaggerates, where I was being "crass" staring at a "very declassé" exhibit on the wall, bare tits on black velvet. She has the neatest vocabulary.

"Crap," she said.

"Huh?"

It was late. The lobby was empty. I'd had a few and I wasn't about to take any crap.

"Crap, crap, crap."

You know how a mouth makes a *puh* sound? And if it's the most wonderful mouth you ever saw in your whole life, you don't give a damn what it says just so it says it? The point being, she could've tied me to a stake and said crap all night right in my face if she wanted to. And she had eyes that could see around corners. Vivian Van Alden eyes, only Chinese.

"I think it's pretty goddamn overwhelming," I said. Something clever.

"Obviously. You've been slack-jawed for ten minutes."

Hardly. She's not always right. I'd been celebrating, that's all, my transfer for one thing, and a toilet I found for another, on the base at Pearl, where if you time it right, about three A.M., you can go into the end stall and sing the "Hawaiian War Chant" if you want to. Or think. Or even roll up little pieces of toilet paper and balance them on your knee, if that's the mood you're in, and flick them against a real door that locks, without someone thinking you're an insane person. Or poke around for the clap. Till dawn, if the truth be known. Gippy says the way I was going about it in Japan it would've been easier to catch over the phone. But I digress. I also got into this annoying habit of practicing chastity every night at Don the Beachcomber's, where all the hot-looking tourists hang out. Gippy says that's like chewing on the box that the candy comes in. So I ambled over to the Moana for a change of pace and wound up staring at all these nipples on the wall, about sixteen of 'em. I probably was a little slack-jawed.

"You look so naked," she said. "What's your name, honey?"

My mom calls me that.

"Peter," I said.

"Well, Peter"—she took a drag on that foot-long holder she loves to trot out at parties—"they're all crap, take my word for it, 'cuz I painted the motherfuckers in a moment of abject poverty." She could've said she was broke, but no, abject poverty. Don't you love it? "My name's Gippy Chin." We shook hands and she kept mine and looked me square in the eye. "Quality hangs in my living room."

You can imagine.

"Modigliani. See the curve of the hip? Lautrec . . . *le bal* . . . Gauguin. Degas. See how delicate? And Chin. Voilà. G. Chin."

There were a lot of them, all different sizes. Like a gallery I guess. I wasn't feeling very talkative.

"Wow."

"You like?"

"Wow. What's that one?"

"A friend in need."

"Is it a still life?"

"Hardly. Isabel. Unfinished."

"Wow."

"Take off your hat, sailor boy. Toss it on the couch. That's a still life. Come to Mama."

Ever smell fresh oil paint?

You can't describe it.

Gippy said to me one day, "Make a list, honey."

1. All growth takes pain.
2. If you truly live life, you learn everything.
3. Every answer exposes hidden questions.

And that's just partial.

The point being, we have company for dinner every Saturday night. (She makes a mean Stroganoff.) And I don't understand half of what they talk about. They're Bohemians, and only about the smartest people I've ever met. Sam, for instance, told me that my childhood was an exercise in futility. I wrote that one down. And Sumi constantly refers to Harriet as that jaded harridan. God, I wish I could talk like that. I'm going to make it a point. Who knows what a harridan is. I think it's from opera. Anyway, the first time she said it, I looked at Gippy—helplessly, I guess—and she patted my hand and said, "Cunt, honey."

I do yak on, though, it's not as if I just listen. They're very unselfish that way, although Isabel says selfishness is the only rational criterion by which to live. I wrote it down, but did she ever get hell from Miles. He says that's her problem, and she says read Korzybski, and he says read Aquinas. (I wonder whatever happened to old Doc.) And they usually settle it with a fencing match through the whole house and out into the street. Over couches and everything. The neighbors hate us. Up theirs. You know what Sam said? That kneeling in a corner on raw rice reminded him of—and everybody yelled at the top of their voices—at once "the Marquis de Sade." I don't know who he is either, but Gippy rubbed my neck and damn near made me cry. But I was too busy working on my list. The other night, to give you an idea how crazy we all are, they took a vote and it was unanimous—I abstained—that taking a "golden opportunity" to look up somebody's bathing suit now and again was perfectly normal behavior. "Or better," Gippy said, and I started to agree, but hold the thought, she said, and we'll talk about it later.

Guess how long it's been since I've been to Confession. Forever.

I did go to Mass, though, about six months ago, and tried to offer it up for Nonna, but it didn't work.

"From what you've told me about your grandmother I hardly think it's her metier to hang around purgatory in a housedress, waiting for you to send her a whatchamacallit."

"Plenary indulgence."

"Yeah. But try it, baby, what've you got to lose?"

Did you ever have a foot rub? Gippy gives the best.

So I went one Sunday to St. Augustine's over on Ohua

Street and I did a few things I never thought I'd do in a million years. First, I tried to say a prayer to the Blessed Virgin, asking her to intercede—that's the way they do it—on Nonna's behalf. Then I wondered. Why do they do it that way anyway? Obviously, the old mind was playing tricks on me because I started thinking maybe the Blessed Virgin needs to feel included, too. Sacrilegious, I'm sure, and that's when the shit hit the fan. I went to Communion, Mr. One-track Sinner, *without going to Confession.* Try it. Try being the only person at the communion rail who's not in the state of sanctifying grace. Pinocchio. And on the way back to my pew I bit it. The host. I actually bit it. Not like you'd bite an apple. I didn't want to go too far. I nibbled on it as if it were a chocolate chip cookie. Nothing happened. Naturally. I mean my mouth didn't fill up with blood or anything, but then instead of singing "O Lord, I Am Not Worthy" under my breath, which is my natural tendency, I bowed my head and started to hum "Singin' in the Rain." Doesn't that beat all? It almost never rains in Hawaii—once in a while a little squall that sneaks up on you and soaks everything in sight for about twenty minutes. "Just long enough to make you change your plans," Gippy says, and I hummed it all the way home like I was Donald O'Connor or somebody.

"Well, it did work in a way then, didn't it?" Gippy said, so I told her about how Nonna used to smell like fresh garlic and face powder, and how dumb Bonnie hid under the stove and crazy Nard tried to put her tail under the rocker and how we all laughed, and a lot of other memories, and then I shoved her onto the couch, playfully, not hard, and gave *her* a nice foot rub for a change.

"Yes," she said. "Oh yes."

Gippy encourages me to write coincidences.

Oh my
Yes
Higher honey
Kiss
Easy
Yes
A little
Soft
Yes
Oh
My
Yes
Sweet
Sweet
Jesus.

She says, *entre nous*, I'm getting a little sophisticated.

We haven't talked about it yet, but I get discharged next month. Here's my plan. Back to college, that's for sure, because you really need a college education to get anywhere these days. "Get wet with life," Gippy says, and the University of Hawaii is only ten minutes away. So I've decided to stay right here in paradise, and we'll get married and I'll go to work for the *Honolulu Advertiser*, the big newspaper here. We don't have to have any kids or anything if she doesn't want to. So tonight I'm going to spin a little Brubeck, light a couple of candles, apropos of nothing—ha-ha—and bring a snifter of Rémy and tell her I love her. Not that I haven't told her before, but it's different when you're not making love and you just touch somebody's face and say it. . . .

XXII ◆◆◆◆◆◆◆◆◆◆◆◆◆◆

"**D**okoni *toire ga arimasuka, dozo,*" I said.

"Isn't that cute," Midge said. "That's so *cute*." Then to my dad. "Isn't that cute, honey?"

"*Ma-che* cute! (Gimme a break!)" Then he said to me, "Pass your plate over here for chrissake." Long time.

"What's it mean, Peter?" said Midge. "I can't wait!"

"Please bring me two toilets." I was being charming.

"That's *darling*! Isn't that darling, honey?"

"White meat or dark meat or both?"

"Both."

"Say it again."

"Two toilets."

"No. In Japanese, silly."

"Dokoni toire ga . . ."

"Too cute for words."

". . . arimasuka, dozo."

"A riot! Tell me all about the girls in Japan. Don't they have the cutest figures? Like little dolls. I'll bet you were a big hit with those shoulders. Honey, give me one *teensy* piece of white meat . . . no, too much, honey . . . *half* that . . . no, half *that*, honey . . . *purr-fect*. Do they all have slant eyes, because my hairdresser's Japanese, she'll *die* over you, and her eyes are almost like mine. Like ours. Tell me about the girls in Hawaii."

"They're quite different. I'm stuffed. Dad, is there any more cranberry?"

"Oho!"

"I think those little grass skirts are *divine*. They're very dark-complected, aren't they, the Hawaiians?"

"They're different, I mean from each other. From one another."

"Is there a lot of intermarriage over there?"

"Uh-huh."

"Did they go crazy for you? Tell the truth."

"Entre nous?"

"Huh?"

"Well . . . that's plenty, Dad . . . I pretty much dated one person the whole time."

"The truth comes out," said Midge. "Hear that, honey? The awful truth comes out. Was she darling?"

"Gippy O'Brien."

"Oh! Please! Irish girls are *darrrling*!"

Know what else is *darrrling*? Maple furniture. Throw-up time. And with orange cushions yet. To match her hair, I guess. The whole apartment is cute as a bug's ear, and my dad doesn't fit in any of it, let alone his new favorite chair. Why did he marry her in the first place? I wonder. Her looks, that's why. A rich ecru might be nice. Nubby maybe. A little less declassé. But bright orange? Come on. I could teach her a few things. How to talk, for one. It's dark com*plexioned*, not dark com*plected*. I think. Anyway, it sounds better. And the pictures on the wall. Two identical subcretinous Scotty dogs staring at each other across a phony fireplace. Art. She pushes him around, too. I'll bet. When they're alone probably. He doesn't have to take that crap from anybody. I peeked in the bedroom while she was putting the finishing touches on her makeup, only because I thought she was dead. I knocked first, of course, and guess what? Even the bed's cute. Wouldn't you know. I know why they got married. The restaurant business is booming, that's why, and she loves to shop and dress up and go to the races, and sit at the bar at the Villa with her girlfriends—every one of them a bug's ear in her own right—and talk about Frank Sinatra and Ava Gardner and other important events. They have absolutely nothing in common.

I wonder if she's *darrrling* in the sack.

I do.

How 'bout them apples?

Which makes me think I'm going bananas, along with the fact that Miss Gippy O'Brien finally got around to answering my first seven letters. It took her an eon practically. "*Dear* Peter." Not *dearest* even. And forget "I miss you, I want you, I love you." I got news items. Who does she think she is, somebody's mother? I almost broke a finger opening it, too. And sniffed the envelope for a trace of oil paint, I'm over the edge, getting soaking wet with life—at U.C. Berkeley, of all places, which is full of *kids* who *refuse* to discuss *anything* important.

"You're gay bait," Doc said, looking up from his wine and around the bar as if he had everybody pegged. He did, too. No wonder. He's getting his master's in philosophy. Finally somebody I can talk to. And thank God he got himself a pair of decent glasses and lost a little weight. Quite a bit actually.

"What does that mean?" I asked him.

That's a thing I find myself doing. I know what gay bait is. Who doesn't, who's got a shred of sophistication? I should've just smiled and said thank you. But no, instead I sat up straighter, no pun intended, in the booth, and spread my shoulders a little. Because I tend to stretch out compliments is why. (Gippy said it's not a huge problem and I'll outgrow it as soon as I become a *declared entity*.) Or something. Who cares.

"Take it as a compliment," Doc said. The Pale Horse Bar. Jesus.

"Why do they call it gay, anyway?" I asked him, sincerely enough, because I've always wondered.

"I'm queer, shall we put it that way?"

Well. I wish he hadn't.

It was like dimming the lights.

I started to feel queer. For Doc. Not queer for Doc. But queer. For Doc, in my stomach. He's supposed to be gay and he feels queer, and I'm supposed to be at least delighted to see him after all these years, and I feel queer, too. It's not my favorite word in the dictionary, for one thing, and for another, who needs to be reminded of that jaded harridan when a person's having an otherwise nice reunion.

And he had this frozen grin on his face. Surprise, surprise. Some bombshell.

"I know," I said wisely, and I haven't even taken Philosophy 1-A.

"Oh, really?" He looked at me mock-shocked and sounded a little British in the bargain.

"I didn't *know*. I just wondered, that's all."

"Yes, well, my friend," he said, "don't knock it if you haven't tried it."

Now see, that's where you get misunderstood. I wasn't knocking it at all. Isabel Han was a little gay, I think, now and then, and remember Toots? And certainly Gippy's had a lot of interesting experiences all over the place, so the last thing I was doing was knocking anything new. Some people are so sensitive. On the other hand I haven't tried crucifixion either.

"How long's it been since your last confession?" I asked him, trying to lighten the moment. I wanted to touch him. "Jeez, remember the nine First Fridays?"

"Shall we drink a toast to Father Wycoff!" he roared, making a broad gesture.

So we did, and we reminisced for a little while about the old Hudson and he gave me a lecture on Adlai Stevenson. But he wouldn't let me hug him good night.

Hi!

Long time no hear! Guess what! I think I can save enough $ to come home for Easter vacation! Ta-da! So let me know, okay? Aloha Oe! Enclosed please find crass article guess who wrote for the Cal Pelican, *the campus humor magazine (so-called) . . . a sidesplitting exposé of my receding (slightly) hairline, all growth takes pain (ha-ha), so let me know, okay? Please tell me. . . .*

HOW MANY TIMES DO YOU HAVE TO BE TOLD? LUNKHEAD! HOW MANY? ONCE *SHOULD BE ENOUGH! BUT NO, NOT YOU, YOU HAVE TO BE TOLD AGAIN AND AGAIN AND AGAIN! AND YOU* STILL *DON'T GET IT THROUGH THAT THICK*

*SKULL OF YOURS! AND STOP LOOKING AT YOUR
HAIR, YOU SPEND ENTIRELY TOO MUCH TIME
IN FRONT OF THE MIRROR, BIG SHOT, AND GET
THAT SULLEN EXPRESSION OFF YOUR FACE!
DON'T YOU* DARE *GIVE ME THAT INNOCENT EX-
PRESSION!* WHAT'S ALL THIS KLEENEX DOING
IN THE WASTEBASKET?

So I started dating Muffy Daley, this Tri-Delt I ran into
at Sather Gate. Which is where you meet the best-
looking girls at Cal because it's the most popular en-
trance to the university. She was walking right toward
me, nude of course (I haven't changed that much), wearing a light blue cashmere sweater. Snug, with a V-neck
and a dark brown skirt, also snug, and Capezios, which
are Italian I think, and which you don't have to wear
any bobby socks with at all, because if you have the
best legs, probably in the entire Republican party, it
makes them even better. We didn't actually meet at
Sather Gate. (Picking up girls is hardly my métier.) We
got acquainted at the gate, where I told her she had the
deepest blue eyes I'd ever seen, cobalt, and invited her
for coffee. Muffy and I first met in Public Opinion 305.
She says I have no values.

XXIII ••••••••••••••

And now the sauce (for two):

Ravioli for three hundred, sauce for two.

1. Several cloves of garlic. The more the merrier.
2. Olive oil.
3. Three very ripe tomatoes.
4. One can tomato sauce. Not the small size, not the large size—the middle size.
5. Plenty of hot red pepper. (The flakes are easiest.)

"Jennifer was a bit of a flake, wasn't she, Mom, when you come right down to it?"

"Who, honey?"

"Jen."

"God. That one. I don't exactly know what you young people mean by a flake, honey, but in my day we said bitch with a capital *B*. And she pushed you around, honey."

"You said."

"You don't have to take that crap from anybody."

"I know. We talked about it this morning."

"Ray noticed it right away. He was something else, wasn't he, that Ray? Did your father like her? You never said."

"He liked the way she talked."

"Well, wasn't Harriet a flake? Face it. Nothing against your father, honey, but what does that tell you?"

"I have to go shopping again."

"And the other one. What was her name?"

"Midge."

"Christ. That one. She thought your father had money, honey, I know because I ran into a friend of her sister's at the City of Paris—"

"So, I'm on my way back to Gelson's. . . . "

"Go, honey. Go. Don't let me rattle on. God, don't you hate it when you forget something on your list? Or worse yet, when the checker leaves it out of the bag. I go right back to the Safeway and I say, 'Listen, young man, you rang this item up . . .' and honey, it could be anything, twenty cents' worth of toothpicks, it's the principle involved, 'Listen, young man, you rang this up and it was *not* in my bag when I got home.' Right between the eyes. They're usually very nice about it. Always look for the Asian checker, honey. Because they're careful. Notice how *careful* the Asians are when they're packing groceries. That's why they're going to take us over, honey. They're *careful*. And, honey, save your receipts."

What the hell do I need here?

Garlic, olive oil—got that. Three toms very ripe, one can tom sauce, not the small, not the large. The medium and . . .

Hot pepper flakes.

Cracks me up.

"That was unfair!" yelled the buttinsky from upstairs.

"What's unfair, and who asked you?"

"To enlist your own mother to corroborate a character assassination."

"Oh, please."

"Well?"

"Aren't we being a tad dramatic?"

"That's exactly what you did."

"Okay. *Not* flaky. *Saucy.* Happy?"

"Who's the flake here is the question."

"Up yours! And we didn't actually meet *under a table* either."

"I know. Over it, and got acquainted under it."

"So?"

"What does that tell you?"

"What, if you're so goddamn smart?"

"That you think with your guess what!"

"Oh, gimme a break!"

"Well?"

"Just picture it for a goddamn minute, and suspend judgment, if that's possible. Here's this *nun,* Sister Mary Jennifer, for chrissake, wearing super-glossy frosty lipstick, drinking a Scotch, passing a joint, pretty heady stuff for an ex-Catholic, paying *no* attention, by the way, to this waif she was with—Howard, I think his name was—who was Wonder Woman, and incidentally monopolizing my date—"

"Who *was?"*

"Golda Meir."

"What a screech. And you were?"

"The Phantom."

"Of course you were."

"Don't make fun."

"Sorry."

"With her hand on my *knee.* And then my *thigh.* Up and down! All over creation! So I started."

"What's a Phantom to do?"

"Do you want to hear this or don't you?"

"If I must."

"Then stop interrupting!"

"........."

"It doesn't matter *who* started. What *possible* difference could it make. Suffice it to say, we had a *very* nice time together. A *saucy* time, if you will. And a *romantic* time, I might add. Yes. Yes. Given the broad definition of the word, I would say so. Sure, our eyes got a little overcast, but through that magic haze they chose a tryst unspoken, albeit half-lidded, to seek and find a comfy place, a cozy nook, where together yet apart, fingers nestled . . ."

"Never have I been so touched."

". . . in that evanescent playground of reverie . . ."

"If you get lyrical again, I'll puke!"

"Fuck you! She was jerking me back to the fifth grade is the point! That's pretty goddamn lyrical stuff on the face of it! Think about it! Sister Mary Boniface, oozing quiet sex—shhhhh—and kindness and love and rosary beads. And Nadine McNulty, for chrissake! Imagine *those* legs at thirty! Not to mention the beautiful Diana, faithful yet somewhat forlorn companion to the Ghost Who Walks, and the *only* person on the face of the earth to know his true identity besides his dog!"

"Kismet."

"Wolf. His name was Wolf. You sure know how to suck the romance out of a good story."

If she had an ounce of brains, she'd be a step ahead of me.

"Yo! Phantom!"

"What now?"

"Check your list."

"What?"

"You forgot the wonton."

"......"

"Get about six hundred."

XXIV········◆

Muffy says if I say f-u-c-k one more time, she'll scream. She will, too. I've had experience. She walks to the middle of the room and clenches her fists and closes her eyes as tight as she can. You should have heard her the other day when she ran out of cigarettes and had to go to the john at the same time. Whoa. Trouble. Except she calls it the *potty*. Then she gets depressed because she thinks she'll get lines in her face before she's thirty. I hope she does. She *tinkles* in the potty. I hate that.

Know what *she* hates?

When I talk about Gippy.

If I'm in the mood to get yelled at, all I have to do is

casually mention how free and talented Gippy Chin is. Especially the free part. Or what a creep Senator Joe McCarthy was. That's another good one. I don't even have to finish my sentence before she starts banging on the dashboard. It's fun. Does that sound crazy? I think it does. That it's actually fun to see Muffy's lips get small and watch her bolt out of the car—she has the neatest figure—and stomp down the street, tossing her head around while I apologize at two miles an hour. Sometimes for ten minutes. I'm sure there's something wrong with me.

Muffy Daley is ticked off. As usual. I told her it was an accident and that I was sorry, but she didn't believe me.

It was, too.

I swear.

Besides, she's a home-ec major, so it had to happen eventually.

Pretty damned ironic when you think about it. All that time I spent in Japan trying to locate the right spot with no success for various reasons, then Hawaii, not getting skilled necessarily. Well, maybe a little, but at least pointed in the right direction. With Muffy it's exactly the opposite. It's an unfair triangle is what it is. I tried, I really did, for months, successfully I might add, *not* to locate the right spot. To *move around* the right spot. Up, down, and miss it on purpose. Jesus. Those are hard rules. And stay interested. Try that one on for size. I don't know anymore. I knew she'd go ape-shit if I ever found it, and sure enough by happenstance not ten minutes ago, and she stomped out of here with a knife between her eyes. I'll call her in a minute.

I'm also a little ticked, frankly.

First of all, she never lets me do special stuff, which I find disappointing because she's one of the most popular girls on campus. And forget *her* doing special stuff. Nevah hoppen, Joe. It hurts, too. Let's be real here. Do I ever mention that to her over coffee? Gee, Muffy, my dick hurts? Not on your life, even though *she* criticizes constantly. Not exactly your barrel of monkeys. Rub-a-dub-dub for an eon. Practically. So she can go *uh*!

Better than nothing, Petey.

It is.

I guess.

It was not entirely my fault either.

She zigged and I zagged, that's all.

I'll give her about five minutes to get home, and I'll call.

I'm also damned sick and tired of doing it at night with every light in the universe off. I like to see stuff. I admit it.

"Stop looking at my place! Honestly!"

Like I'm perverted or something. Face it, it's a very pretty place.

The only reason Miss Daley condescended to rub today, before God the Father turned Berkeley pitch-black, is that it's midterms and she nailed an *A* in cinnamon rolls or some damn thing, and it's pouring outside, and I live closer to the campus than she does, and I told her that I had a present for her.

I accept half the responsibility.

I'll call in a half hour.

I don't even remember why I bought her the perfume in the first place, but that's what started the proceedings.

To apologize for something.

What?

Saturday night.

I said to her, "Muff, you sure look dynamite in that sweater." The cerise job, short sleeves. But what I should've said was, and she kind of simmered for a while before she uncorked, "Muff, that sweater sure looks dynamite on *you*." See the difference? I didn't either at first, but it turns out "You sure look dynamite *in*" something presupposes that you didn't already look dynamite in something else. For instance. Or nothing at all for that matter, make no mistake, whenever I can catch a glimpse. Until you put the sweater *on* is the point. Which technically means that the *sweater* is responsible for making you look dynamite. But if you say, "Muff, that sweater sure looks dynamite on *you*," obviously it means . . .

It means . . .

That the sweater was a piece of pink shit, and one day Muffy Daley threw it on and the sun came up!

Anyway.

I decided to get her something by way of an apology, and on my way to the accessory counter at Capwell's to look for just the right scarf to go with the Sweater Muffy Daley Made Famous, I passed the perfume counter and it hit me like a fresh breeze out of the past. Why are past breezes so fresh?

It was all my fault.

Maybe if she hadn't been facing the wall with all of her might, and squinching her cobalt eyes closed, crevices be damned, like I was begging her to give up atomic secrets or something. Okay. So I got a little bored. Staring into her ear. Counting capillaries and rub-a-dubbing till the cows come home, so I tried to jazz up the situation, that's all, and I purposefully placed my face into her whole neck and took the deepest breath imaginable. . . .

White Shoulders
By
Lah-vah

"I'd adore it," whispered Vonnie Cassidy. So quietly.

Me too.

Boy, did I get hell.

F-u-c-k it, I'll call her in the morning.

Who the hell do I think I am anyway?

There's a good question. And I have a hunch I'm supposed to know the answer is what bothers me.

Muffy says I'm too nice. There's a grain of truth there.

And Gippy says I need to bloom, and by the time I'm forty she'll be a hundred and three. Hardly. Muffy says I'm too intense for her and she's too happy-go-lucky for me, and Gippy says I'm a little sophisticated and Muffy says I'm not nearly the man of the world I think I am, and if I hadn't had that artsy-fartsy, excuse her language, experience in Hawaii, I'd be a real straight arrow.

So?

How come everybody's right?

What I really want to be is terribly sophisticated and agonizingly casual if it kills me. I'm too old to be confused.

Muffy's helping.

We see a lot more of each other since the accident. Mostly we go to the movies and to Mel's Drive-in, where you can sit inside if you want to be noticed. Fine with me. She likes to be noticed, and I like to be noticed with her. We don't disagree on everything. Then back to my room if she doesn't wind up getting annoyed. That's unfair. She doesn't exactly get annoyed, sometimes a little thing, like tonight's *tick-off* was sort of to the world at large. "*Why*? Can anyone explain to me why they spend so much time in movies, opening and closing doors?" It was rhetorical, thank God. She's a damn good student of other people's nonchalance, though, and I mean that sincerely, without sarcasm.

I. *Coffee shop behavior.*

A. *How to sit in a booth.*

How to sit in a booth? See, I appreciate the advice on the one hand and on the other hand, I despise it. But she's right on the money.

1. *Sit back.*

You don't catch James Garner leaning over a table, wrinkling.

2. *Hang left arm leisurely over booth.*

Rock Hudson. "And smile for heaven's sake. Honestly!"

3. *Let that left hand drape.*

Brando.

Muffy says I'm a clumsy Jack Palance, if ever there was such an animal.

Ha.

If she only knew.

She'd have me committed if she only knew.

I am the Phantom.

Not really.

When I'm home in bed. Alone. Naturally. Obviously I don't run around Berkeley with a purple suit and a mask on, saving people from their finals. I do get around, though, over the furniture and through the jungle. Sometimes I'm David Niven, but mostly the Ghost Who Walks.

Jesus Christ, Peter, at twenty-seven, pushing thirty?

They're going to take me away somewhere, I swear, and eat the key, but that's when I'm the coziest.

So?

Who wouldn't be, with the friendly natives well hidden and standing guard outside my cave which is equally well disguised by the surrounding forest, my arms comforting Diana, who is exquisite but almost never right, otherwise why would *I* be the only person in the world to have a secret telephone line to the White House on my side of the bed so I can advise President Eisenhower on surprise attacks. It's hard to explain.

You could have knocked me over with a feather. It weighs a ton. And it's ugly. It looks like a giant dying avocado, plus the capital *P* doesn't work. The guy at the repair shop got all rhapsodic and said that Olympia was the Mercedes-Benz of typewriters. Pretty goddamn rhapsodic if you ask me, the point being why after eighteen months and three days of not even a postcard, does Miss G. Chin, no return address, decide to send me something we used to keep flowers on to pretty up.

"*I'm off to parts unknown . . .*"

What else is new?

"*. . . Aloha, my dreamer. . . .*"

She could've gone all day, believe me. I'm not exactly made out of stone. But what really gets to me is, she sends me *orders*, practically—who the hell is she to send me orders?—to get my ass to Los Angeles after graduation, and to meet some guy who writes scripts, like for movies and TV. Los Angeles! That's only five hundred f-u-c-k-i-n-g miles away.

They had been to the movies. The Swan *with Grace Kelly and Louis Jourdan at the Grand Lake Theatre. Appropriately. He had spilled his popcorn on his lap during an important part and whispered* fuck, *and she had clenched her fists and looked at the ceiling and whispered "honestly!" because there is no screaming at the Grand Lake. Later, in the car, he perceived that she was practicing what she had seen on the silver screen. Regality, serenity, amiability. Part of him welcomed the change, and part of him yearned for her former predictable self. Neither here nor there being his métier, if you will. The part of him that welcomed the change sent his one-track mind reeling carelessly, and decided to join her in make-believe. The other part of him has been pissed off for months.*

Mel's Drive-in. Still later. The regal couple, seated and served.

"You look ravishing, ma chérie, *in that ensemble," said Louis to Grace, part one pronouncing it* on-somb *and accompanying his comment with a crooked grin, her favorite quality in a man, and part two knowing full well that he had said it bass-ackwards again, only this time on purpose.*

Grace stiffened.

What's a part to do?

Part one moved to drape his left arm casually over the top of the booth, and part two whacked his coffee cup on the way up, with such force that the coffee neither glid nor trickled, but fairly shot toward the onsomb. Swan-ish white, beige appliqué. Cream and sugar, too. Part one searched the floor for a pound of raw rice in which to bury his knees, part two became the Hunchback of Notre Dame, pouring lead and ringing bells. One apologized, two giggled.

Grace unraveled.

She easily picked up a ride from a policeman who was a ringer for John Wayne, and both parts of our hero went home and got under the covers.

Part one realizes that marriage is probably out of the question, part two is eating cookies and milk, and very shortly will become William Holden and blow up the bridge on the River Kwai.

I can't get over G. Chin. No return address—who the hell does she think I am anyway?

XXV ◆◆◆◆◆◆◆◆◆◆◆◆◆

So I packed my pillow, and here I am in L.A., of all places. For a little while only. That's definite. I wouldn't have come at all if my mom and Ray weren't here for the Hollywood Park meet. Ray plans to make a fortune, and my mom and I yak it up all day. Anything wrong with a person with my recent history wanting to spend a minute with his mother? I think not. She never criticizes, for one thing. Two weeks should make a new man out of me.

L.A. stinks, my mom says. "Honey, let's face it. The world begins and ends from Sutter to Geary and Grant to Powell. Would you say that I'm a snob? Let's call a spade a steam shovel. Los Angeles *tries* to be sophisticated, honey, but it's neither here nor there."

Just what I need, a city that suits me.

"Wear a suit, honey," she said, and she's right. Ray agreed that I should show a little class, although I didn't bring one along. I hate suits. But how often does one get invited to tea? Nobody in my family. In the Hollywood Hills yet, with a Mr. Ambrose Costello. What a neat name. Leave it to Gippy.

You should see Ray's closet. Six suits, six sports jackets, six pair of slacks, and a half-dozen pair of shoes you could ladle soup with in a pinch. And Ray being right-handed, everything faces to the left so he can grab. Actually he never grabs his clothes; he *removes* them, my mom says, with his right hand so that he can take the edge of the jacket or whatever and the corner of the hanger in his left hand, slip the hanger from the jacket with his right, rehang it, and slide right in. I never thought of it that way before. He also has shoe trees— mahogany, I think—in all of his shoes, and when he takes them off at night, no matter how loaded he is, and puts the trees in, he whacks the shoes, each one just once, outside edge down, on the floor so that the trees will even out. Or something.

My mom's closet is pretty impressive, too, except Ray can't understand why she keeps her right shoe on the left side and her left shoe on the right side.

"How can you live like that?" he said.

She explained it to him. "Ray, it's because I cross my legs when I take my shoes off at night, don'tcha know."

Which is a good point, except as Ray said, "Yeah, but you don't cross your legs when you take your shoes *out* of the closet in the morning." Which is also a good point. So she changed it around.

I may only stay a week.

"We don't want any," yelled a voice from inside the house, whereupon somebody turned off the opera.

"Hi."

"Good afternoon, miss. My name is Peter Russo. I'm here to see Mr. Ambrose Costello. For tea."

"I know, I know, I know. Come on in."

Faded overalls, white T-shirt, bare feet. The child of the house, obviously.

"Just flop anywhere, okay?" she said. "Want a beer?"

Precocious, naturally.

"That would be delightful, miss."

"Amby's at a story conference. Sort of rush-rush, so I'm elected. Isn't that glen plaid a bit much? It's eighty fucking degrees out." Smart-alecky, too. I could swear I heard her cackle from the kitchen. "You want a salami sandwich?"

What a house!

No rooms really. No floor-to-ceiling walls. You could take a tour of the whole place by standing on your tip-toes in the middle of the living room and spinning. And white! Everything was white, except for the art wall. The art wall was grand.

"I love that," I said, pointing to Isabel Han, finished. Sweet Jesus, I thought.

"Wheatena," she said. "Come on, I'll give you a quick tour so you don't have to do *Swan Lake* in the middle of the room." Which put me in mind of my very first nonconformist.

Partitions, that's all, separating everything from everything else.

"Are you Mr. Costello's daughter?"

"Yeah. You may call me Maryanne. And that thing that seems to be captivating you, by the way, is a bidet. *Bee-day,*" she repeated, and looked at me like I was from Fresno. "And if you piss in it, I'll kill you."

"How old are you?" I asked.

"How old do you think I am? And watch your mayonnaise."

"Oops, sorry. Thirteen?"

She cackled.

"Seventeen. It's because I have no tits. Lucky, huh?"

"Mayo in a salami sandwich. Hmmm. Interesting."

"Interesting?"

"Different."

"I think food snobs should be executed."

"Not at all. I was merely remarking."

"You're practically sucking your knuckles. Just eat it and shut up."

Twerp.

And a big bay window the size of Rhode Island, framing a couple of movie studios. Thirteen swimming pools and . . .

"What is that?" I asked, instead of hitting her.

"What?"

"Down there. That big street."

"Sunset Strip. Don't you know anything?"

"I suppose you're a writer, too?"

"I'm a reader."

"The old I'll-lick-you-yet view of Hollywood," I said, pretty damned cleverly.

"You lick it, buster. I'm off to Sarah Lawrence."

I had this dream last night that I was locked in Ray's closet. I was sentenced to be there for twenty years because I got caught in bed with my mom drinking cocoa and taking turns reading *Black Beauty*. Imagine this big hairy guy, right. No wonder. Except all the clothes were mine, but nothing fit, and the jackets were on the wrong hangers with the wrong pants and everything was facing bass-ackwards, and try as I may I couldn't make anything come out even let alone get the mayo off the shoe trees, even though Sarah Lawrence was banging on the dashboard and all I had to do was tell her to turn the knob, but she couldn't hear me. Figure that one out. I'm nowhere to be found is the truth of the matter, a man of many parts. Shall we dance?

Plus I've got a pile of scripts next to my pillow to study if I promise to return them. "A promise made over salami is a fucking oath. Don't you agree?" Like we were best pals or something. I'll probably have to be here for a whole month. The little creep also suggested I better damn well know how my story ends before I start. Christ, I'll never get that one right.

"Jesus Christ," said Dominic. "You got a minute?"

"*Shoot.*"

"I had a dream last night that was so fuckin' real I could touch it. *Midge!*"

"*That one.*"

"Yeah, and she's sittin' on top of my goddamn plant."

"The schefflera."

"Huh?"

"*Harriet's spot.*"

"Yeah. Up there with some guy I never saw before in my life. Whispering. 'I want a nice clean job. No fuss, no muss.'"

"Jesus."

"A hit man for chrissake, I damn near fell outta bed! So I turn on the light. Gone. Christ knows how the hell they got in in the first place. So I turn *off* the light, and I'll be a son of a bitch if they're not right back up there in the goddamn tree, cozy as hell. So. I pretend I'm asleep, and she says to this guy—listen to this—'He's got two grand in stocks. . . .' Now, you're aware that she got a bundle in the divorce."

"Yeah, yeah."

" 'Two grand in stocks, and thirty-one thousand, five hundred, twenty-eight bucks, and seventy-two cents in the Bank of America. Plenty for both of us.' "

"Jesus."

"Goddamn right, I'm still not recovered!"

"They say, though, Dad, that we write our own dreams."

"Oho, tell me. The bank does not give *anybody* that information."

"I mean we compose the plots."

"The hell you say."

"I do it all the time. Whaddya say I come up. I got about fifty ravioli. My fingers are hammered from wonton. I need a break, and we'll sample it together."

"I'm not sure I got that straight. This is a dream?"

"Sort of. But let's do it."

"Hell of a dream."

"Yeah."

"Just the two of us."

"Who knows?"

"Rose?"

"I said *who knows. What'd you say?*"

"You tryin' to fuckin' confuse me. I could've sworn you said Rose."

"I didn't, but she's sure as hell part of the story."

I could hear a Toscano.

"I'll be a son of a bitch. . . . Goddamn . . ." He broke into quiet song. "*What a difference . . . a day makes . . .*" Good voice, too. Emphysema notwithstanding.

So I chimed in.

"*Twenty-four . . . little hours . . .*"

More Toscano.

"Just don't tell her it was my idea."

"Mom."

"Peter, I was just this minute thinking about you. You know how the silliest things can keep you awake at night? Remember yesterday we were talking about how the checker can accidentally leave something out of your shopping bag, and I said it was the principle of the thing, even if it was twenty cents' worth of toothpicks? Can you believe that's what kept me awake? Twenty cents worth of *goddamn* toothpicks. Good luck finding anything these days for twenty cents. The point is, honey, I've had the best of it. Isn't it strange how a little thing like that can keep you awake?"

"I got an idea."

"Tell me, tell me."

I revealed the plot.

"Honey, your father will never agree to that."

M.A.

I'm off to parts unknown. Enclosed find one dozen ravioli in dry ice, against my better judgment. For chrissake hold the pineapple.

P.

XXVI ••••••••••••

Dominic has this little hat. A navy-blue watch cap, the kind sailors wear when rough weather is on the horizon. It hangs on the first hook on the left in his closet so that he can grab with his left, put on with his right, which he did. His cane was another story. He couldn't find the fuckin' thing. So I did, while he packed four Toscani, one at a time, in his left inside jacket pocket—he's right-handed. I simply retraced the steps he'd taken through the door into the apartment after we'd come back from his haircut earlier in the day. I found the cane hanging on the first chair on the right. Naturally.

The cab honked. Dominic thought better of it, went

back to his desk, picked up another cigar, and put it between his teeth. A five-Toscani night.

Rose lives on the second floor of her apartment building out the Marina. An older, no-elevator building, so Dominic and I counted the steps as we climbed. Slowly. Thirty-two in all. "I'll be a son of a bitch," he remarked at the top, since it had been exactly that many years, give or take, since he and Rose had laid eyes on each other and he'd tipped his hat on Market Street.

Rose waited at the door, some ten feet from the landing. He looked up, footing be damned.

"It's Rose, Dad."

"Ah," he said, and thrust his cane at me as if it was a snake.

"Hello, Dom," she said, and extended her hand. She wore beige slacks, well tailored—she's a hell of a seamstress—a maroon silk blouse, and First by Van Cleef & Arpels.

"Hello, Rose," said Dominic as they shook hands. "Goddamn," he added, keeping her hand.

The Phantom, being unaccustomed, studied the carpet.

"Just enough olive oil to cover the bottom of the pan," cautioned Dominic as he watched me pour.

"And make sure the garlic is chopped *very* fine, honey," added Rose.

"What did she say?"

"*Very fine on the garlic,*" I repeated.

"Oho. Essential."

"Your father needs to get his ears washed out, honey."

"Did you chop the tomatoes and mix 'em with the tomato sauce, Mom?"

"Peter, I was making this sauce before you were born. Nonna never said much, but I watched."

"Now," said Dominic. "Gas on very high, but *lift* the pan off the fire so that the garlic sautés to a point where it's golden brown."

"Got it."

"Very critical," he added.

"If you let it burn, honey, it's crap. You might as well throw it in the garbage. Honey, make me another Canadian Club."

"If you let it burn," added Dominic, "you might as well throw the whole fuckin' thing in the garbage."

"Why does your father have to use that word, of all words?"

"Canadian Club comin' up."

"I thought he was more intelligent than that."

"Pete, for chrissake, pay attention here. Now. Place the pan back onto the hot gas and add the tomato mixture . . . not yet . . . not yet . . . golden brown, *capisce?*"

"Your grandmother never made quite a production of it, I must say."

"*Very* critical," said Dominic. "*Now!*"

I poured.

"*Maritata!*" cried Dominic triumphantly as the tomatoes hit the hot olive oil and golden-brown garlic, some of it splashing onto the stove, the wall. A splotch here, a still life there.

"That means the *marriage*, honey. That's what they call it when the sauce goes all over the place like that. The *marriage*."

Plenty of hot red pepper flakes, it was decided, gives it that extra bite.

They couldn't remember when the ravioli came so good.

I could.

Boy, could I ever, and part of me wanted to dive into yesterday, ingredient by ingredient, as I felt a certain layer of sentiment, only natural, spread over me like hot fudge.

"*Yuk!*" yelled a familiar voice from five hundred miles away, upstairs.

"Huh?"

"*The last thing you need tonight is a rich dessert.*"

"Yeah, but . . ."

"*What's the other part of you want to do?*"

"I don't know, wise guy, you tell me."

"*Hush up.*"

"Those days are gone," I heard Dominic say as I came out of the john. "*Nobody* delivers anymore."

"And try and find a highball for fifty cents," added Rose.

The best butcher in town, though, they agreed, is still at Petrini's on Masonic and Fulton. And the Royal Bakery out the Mission is tops since the Parisian, between Powell and Stockton, went out of business.

Mrs. Bertotti's daughter's boy, it turns out—Guido with the cock eyes—inherited a big corner house on Chestnut Street,

"A marmeluke, if there ever was one."

"A real good-for-nothing."

Al Jolson is gone forever, Mother Nature is here to stay, and nothing clogs up a drain like lamb fat.

They also agreed that *Sailor Boy, Sailor Boy* was probably the best screenplay I ever wrote, although *Angora Woman* did better since they let me direct. I was paid a hundred thousand to walk away from the project.

"And tell your father to get rid of that Colace, honey. *Stewed prunes, Dom*, pitless, right out of the box, boil water, pour it over, leave uncovered till cool. Simple. I never had an irregular day in my life."

"Sometimes a little twist of lemon," added Dominic.

"Honey, make me another Canadian Club, light this time, honey, and tell your father Proposition H, for God's sake, although I must say I never had a hemorrhoid. *I had a Cadillac.*"

Dominic went to the john.

"He should use his cane at all times, honey."

Rose went to the john.

"I hope you have half her spirit when you're eighty-five."

"Don't *ever* divulge that recipe," Dominic ordered, shaking a crooked finger, as we stood at the door and I handed him his cane.

"Or leave something out, honey. What they don't know won't give 'em a headache. And tell your father for chrissake to get rid of that hat."

XXVII ....

I'*ve had better* was the message on my answering machine. *But why don't you just send me the recipe immediately and I'll see if I can fix it.*

I returned her call immediately. "You're not getting it, Maryanne." This time I sang it.

"You're sort of a dope or something, aren't you, Petey?"

"I promised my family."

"You're the only person in the world who gets mawkish over fucking ravioli."

"I'll give you a few more. Settle for that."

"Kind of pathetic, aren't you?"

"Just eat 'em and shut up, ha-ha-ha."

"You are such an asshole."

"Jesus."

"What?"

"I was just thinking . . ."

"God save us."

"How long have we known each other, anyway?"

"Since the fucking pyramid days. We were on a rock pile together."

"Seems like it."

"And I'm the only thing that stands between you and a mental ward."

I have this thing about the past.

"I'll think about it," I said.

Cackle, cackle, cackle. "I should marry you, I could pussy-whip you so bad."

"*So?*" asked the upstairs oracle.

"So what?"

"*So cough it up and leave something out. That's all.*"

"It's two typewritten pages! Single-spaced!"

"*I suggest the calf brains.*"

"What?"

"*To leave out.*"

"I already did."

"*There you go.*"

"I haven't the words to tell you how good it feels to get this cover off."

"Get used to it. This is the longest recipe in the world."

"Whooops, what's that thing you're slipping inside me?"

"Paper, wiseass."

"Oooooh . . . my God . . . Jesus . . ."

"You're kidding."

"No . . . really . . . space me . . . yes . . . there . . . there . . . now . . . quick . . . adjust my tabs. . . ."

"Like this?"

"Yes . . . yes . . . straighten my edge. . . ."

"Better?"

"Higher . . . yes . . . dot . . . space . . . . comma . . . dot . . . dot . . . God . . . *oh . . . my . . . dot . . .*"

"Oh, please!"

"*My keys . . . my crevices . . .*"

My ass

You get lyrical

I go shopping

Who said that

I did

Which part

What difference

Entre nous

Make a list, honey.

1. 1½ pounds boneless veal.
2.

TITLES OF THE AVAILABLE PRESS
in order of publication

*Available in a Ballantine Mass Market Edition.

little pictures, short stories by Andrew Ramer
THE IMMIGRANT: A Hamilton County Album, a play by Mark Harelik
HOW THE DEAD LIVE, a mystery by Derek Raymond*
BOSS, a novel by David Handler*
THE TUNNEL, a novel by Ernesto Sabato
FOR FOREIGN STUDENT, a novel by Philippe Labro, translated by William R. Byron*
ARLISS, a novel by Llya Allen
THE CHINESE WESTERN: Short Fiction from Today's China, translated by Zhu Hong*
THE VOLUNTEERS, a novel by Moacyr Scliar
LOST SOULS, a novel by Anthony Schmitz
SEESAW MILLIONS, a novel by Janwillem van de Wetering
SWEET DIAMOND DUST, a novel by Rosario Ferré
SMOKEHOUSE JAM, a novel by Lloyd Little
THE ENGIMATIC EYE, short stories by Moacyr Scliar
THE WAY IT HAPPENS IN NOVELS, a novel by Kathleen O'Connor
THE FLAME FOREST, a novel by Michael Upchurch
FAMOUS QUESTIONS, a novel by Fanny Howe
SON OF TWO WORLDS, a novel by Haydn Middleton
WITHOUT A FARMHOUSE NEAR, a nonfiction by Deborah Rawson
THE RATTLESNAKE MASTER, a novel by Beaufort Cranford
BENEATH THE WATERS, a novel by Oswaldo França, Júnior
AN AVAILABLE MAN, a novel by Patric Kuh
THE HOLLOW DOLL (A Little Box of Japanese Shocks), by William Bohnaker
MAX AND THE CATS, a novel by Moacyr Scliar
FLIEGELMAN'S DESIRE, a novel by Lewis Buzbee
SLOW BURN, a novel by Sabina Murray
THE CARNAL PRAYER MAT, by Li Yu, translated by Patrick Hanon
THE MAN WHO WASN'T THERE, by Pat Barker
I WAS DORA SUAREZ, a mystery by Derek Raymond
LIVE FROM EARTH, a novel by Lance Olsen
THE CUTTER, a novel by Virgil Suarez
ONE SUMMER OUT WEST, a novel by Philippe Labro, translated by William R. Byron.
THE CHRIST OF THE BUTTERFLIES, a novel by Ardythe Ashley
CHINESE POETRY: Through the Words of the People, edited by Bonnie McCandliss

*Available in a Ballantine Mass Market Edition.